Dear Reader,

Here's the fourth and last in the series THE MONTANA MALONES, which debuted June '97 with *A Marriage Made in Joeville,* followed in December by *The Best Little Joeville Christmas* and *Last of the Joeville Lovers,* May '98.

Thanks for the many wonderful letters from readers asking that this series continue—I couldn't help but respond. In *The Unknown Malone* it's seven years later and you will get to know more about Taylor's brother, Michael, along with the woman he can't resist, Nicole— a woman on the run with a storehouse of secrets.

Familiar faces return for an encore: Savannah and Ryder, Jenny and Shane, Taylor and Josh, Max, Hannah and, of course, Billy, whom many of you have said touched your hearts from beginning to end. Also by request, one of these other characters finds romance, too.

As always, I enjoy hearing from readers and welcome your letters.

Here's hoping you have a happy and loving holiday season!

Warmest regards,

Anne Eames

Anne Eames

Dear Reader,

Welcome to Silhouette Desire—where you're guaranteed powerful, passionate and provocative love stories that feature rugged heroes and spirited heroines who experience the full emotional intensity of falling in love!

This October you'll love our new MAN OF THE MONTH title by Barbara Boswell, *Forever Flint*. Opposites attract when a city girl becomes the pregnant bride of a millionaire outdoorsman.

Be sure to "rope in" the next installment of the exciting Desire miniseries TEXAS CATTLEMAN'S CLUB with *Billionaire Bridegroom* by Peggy Moreland. When cattle baron Forrest Cunningham wants to wed childhood friend Becky Sullivan, she puts his love to an unexpected test.

The always-wonderful Jennifer Greene returns to Desire with her magical series HAPPILY EVER AFTER. *Kiss Your Prince Charming* is a modern fairy tale starring an unforgettable "frog prince." In a sexy battle-of-the-sexes tale, Lass Small offers you *The Catch of Texas*. Anne Eames continues her popular miniseries MONTANA MALONES with *The Unknown Malone*. And Sheri WhiteFeather makes her explosive Desire debut with *Warrior's Baby,* a story of surrogate motherhood with a twist.

Next month, you'll really feel the power of the passion when you see our new provocative cover design. Underneath our new covers, you will still find six exhilarating journeys into the seductive world of romance, with a guaranteed happy ending!

Enjoy!

Joan Marlow Golan
Senior Editor, Silhouette Desire

Please address questions and book requests to:
Silhouette Reader Service
U.S.: 3010 Walden Ave., P.O. Box 1325, Buffalo, NY 14269
Canadian: P.O. Box 609, Fort Erie, Ont. L2A 5X3

THE UNKNOWN MALONE
ANNE EAMES

SILHOUETTE *Desire*®

Published by Silhouette Books
America's Publisher of Contemporary Romance

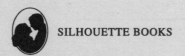 SILHOUETTE BOOKS

ISBN 0-373-76247-X

THE UNKNOWN MALONE

Visit us at www.romance.net

Printed in U.S.A.

Books by Anne Eames

Silhouette Desire

*The Montana Malones

ANNE EAMES

This is Anne Eames's seventh novel for Desire. She has been a Golden Heart finalist and Maggie winner, and her books have appeared on the *USA Today* bestseller list.

Anne and her husband, Bill, live in southeastern Michigan.

You may write to Anne Eames at: 4217 Highland, Box #252, Waterford, MI 48328. For an autographed gift, please enclose a business-length, self-addressed, stamped envelope.

To Tim, Emily, Haley, TJ,
Savannah and Tom Garthe
with all my love always
and
with special thanks to
forester extraordinaire,
Betsy Couzens Mitton

One

At a gas station east of Livingston, Montana, about forty miles from Joeville, Nicole Bedder leaned closer to the rest room mirror and growled in frustration. The false eyelash she'd so carefully glued in place was now stuck to the end of her finger. It didn't help that her hands were shaking. It had been eighteen hours since her last meal.

She tried again, this time using tweezers to press the phony lashes to her own. With more finesse it worked, and she applied the second. They felt heavy and she blinked hard as she riffled through her purse for blush.

A loud knock on the door made her jump.

"I'll be out in a sec."

She'd already ratted and sprayed her recently bleached hair into a style even Dolly Parton would have been proud of. Now she applied a thick layer of red lipstick over her already full lips, making sure she exceeded the lines in a suitable fashion.

She stepped back and inspected the finished product. The denim skirt wasn't as short as most, the top not very tight, but sexy things had never been part of her wardrobe. This would just have to do.

A quick readjustment inside her bra and the cleavage atop her red tank top swelled. She turned from side to side for one last look.

Good grief. Who was this person?

Before she could lose her nerve she thrust open the door. The plump, elderly woman waiting outside gasped. Her eyes traveled the length of the young woman in front of her before her lips settled into a firm, straight line. She brushed passed Nicole with a disgusted humph and there was a resounding twist of the lock behind her.

A feeling of dread spread across Nicole's shoulders and neck and she fought a sudden urge to cry. Obviously she had just convinced somebody's grandma that she was a worldly woman, but could she trick the owner of the Purple Palace?

Yet all she had to do was fit in, she reminded herself. A helper, the ad had said. Yesterday she'd decided she couldn't go to a place like that looking like Marian the Librarian, her normally mousy brown hair tied in its familiar ponytail. No, she had to look as though the occupants' shenanigans were nothing out of the ordinary, that they weren't the least bit offensive to her sensibilities.

Now, with hands on hips, she looked to the sky and shook her head. High school drama classes hadn't prepared her for this gig. But what choice did she have? She said a quick prayer, filled her lungs and then strode toward the gas pump, trying not to wobble on her Salvation Army high heels.

The hood was up on her rusted green Chevy. The mechanic wiped his hands on a greasy rag and did a double take in her direction. When he closed his mouth, he saun-

tered over, pretending he hadn't noticed her transformation
in the rest room.

"A couple belts are pretty old and cracked. Don't think
they'll make it much longer." He was staring at her chest
and she wanted to smack him upside the head. Instead, she
practiced a confident voice.

"Will they make it another forty miles?"

"Hard to say. Maybe yes, maybe no."

She looked at the pump: $14.78. She didn't have to
check her purse to know. Inside was a ten, a five and some
change.

"Guess I'll take my chances."

He cocked his head to one side and continued wiping his
filthy hands, his lopsided grin making it pretty clear he'd
consider a trade. Fingers shaking, she retrieved the bills
from her purse and slapped them in his blackened palm.

"Suit yourself, ma'am." He shrugged and walked back
to the front of the car and slammed the hood down.

She was tempted to leave without the change, but
twenty-two cents was twenty-two cents. When he returned
with it, she flashed him a smile and drove off—stomach
growling, engine knocking and nerve dwindling by the second.

Michael Phillips chuckled under his breath, riding atop
his first and only mare—an old workhorse named Mae. Her
slow waddle up the hillside and across the ridge was adding
an extra half hour to the trip to his sister's neighboring
farm, but the delay would be well worth it.

He couldn't wait to see the expression on Taylor's face
when she saw him...here...in Montana...and heard what
he had done. If he'd driven his van she might have seen
him coming. After months of planning and secrecy, he
wanted to milk the moment for all it was worth.

He stopped where the trail cut to the west and let Mae

nibble at low-hanging brush while his eyes scanned the rolling countryside below.

And there she was. On her knees in the flower beds in front of the old blue farm house, one he hadn't seen in seven years. The only notable change were the two little ones who played close by. His heart was in his throat. He'd missed his niece's and nephew's early years, but now he was here, and he planned to make up for it. He tugged on Mae's reins and she loped on.

He rode closer until Mae started nickering, then he tethered her to a tree and hiked the rest of the way, excitement building with every step. Finally he broke into an easy jog, darting behind trees until he came alongside the old familiar house. He paused a moment, caught his breath and then ambled around the corner, his hands thrust deep in his pockets, his grin no longer controllable.

Two-year-old Emily spotted him first and ran to her mother, peeking shyly from the far side. Soon-to-be-six John stopped playing with his truck and stood. "Mama?"

Taylor rocked back on her knees, swiped a muddy glove across her forehead and then nearly toppled over as she let out a yelp. "Michael!"

He ran to her and swooped her up, spinning her around. "Hi, sis." When he set her down they were both laughing and crying at the same time.

"When did you—" She glanced around. "How did you—" She flung her arms around his neck again. "Oh, Michael. It's so good to see you. How long can you stay?"

Emily and John stood a safe distance behind their mother, not knowing what to make of it all. He smiled and gave them a conspiratorial wink.

"Hmm…with a little luck…oh, I'd say another sixty years or so."

She fell back a step, her mouth agape—just the reaction he'd hoped for.

"I bought the Purple Palace."

Her eyes widened. "You *what?*"

"Yep. Lock, stock and ol' Mae."

"Mae?"

"Their only horse."

"Let me get this straight. You sold the family business."
He nodded. "And you bought the Purple Palace." He nodded again. "And you plan to—" She rolled her hand in a
fast-forward motion.

"Work the place."

"Work the place. As in—" She glanced over her shoulder at the children and didn't finish, her sudden frown saying it all.

It was time to end the ruse. "As in restoring it. It's a
grand old lady—old enough to become a historical land-
mark."

"And the…girls?"

"Bought them out. They've all moved on to greener pas-
tures."

Taylor's smile turned into a large grin, and then the
sounds of their laughter echoed across the valley.

When the adults composed themselves, the children
came forward one at a time and met Uncle Mike, their little
smiles exposing various stages of teeth, their eyes wide
with excitement. They walked hand in hand inside for lemonade and for as much catching up as the clock would
allow. Michael was expecting a load of lumber and drywall,
and he didn't want to miss the truck. And there was the
possibility that someone would answer his ad for a helper,
too. After an hour he left, promising to return for supper
at six.

The pink exterior and the purple trim were peeling in
places, but Nicole had to admit the big old place had a lot
of charm. If only it weren't—

On a nervous sigh, she bracketed her hands around her eyes and peered into a window, seeing no signs of life on the other side. She'd knocked hard enough to wake the dead, but no one came to the ornate oval oak door. Were they all upstairs sleeping—getting ready for a busy night? Or could Tuesday be a day off?

Her stomach lurched, and she didn't think it was from hunger. How could she ever work at a place like this? Again she reminded herself she had no choice. Besides, she was only applying for "helper"—whatever that meant. Hostess, maybe? Clean ashtrays? Freshen drinks? Wash lingerie? She wrinkled her nose.

It didn't matter. She'd do whatever it took. She had to.

If only she'd learned more about the job. The little she knew about it she'd overheard yesterday. Dire straits and creative problem solving had driven her to a local doughnut shop where she'd ordered one doughnut hole and a glass of water, and waited for someone to discard a newspaper so that she could scour the employment section. Before it came to that, a pair of old-timers sitting next to her started laughing about the Purple Palace's ad: Helper. No experience needed.

"Wonder what a helper would do there?" one had asked.

The other hunched his shoulders, then started laughing louder.

It was at that very moment Nicole had decided what she'd do, even though each time she allowed herself to dwell on it, as was the case now, her pulse began to race.

What if the...ladies...felt better about themselves when they thought they were...helping? Could a helper be—?

No! The ad couldn't be for *that*. She cringed, pushing aside the possibility. It had to be for something else. Exactly what seemed irrelevant since she was short on options and long on responsibilities. Besides, unemployment was on the rise again, now that that Hollywood production company had left the area. As long as their movie was being shot at that ranch to the north, there had been extra work in motels and restaurants. Now the locals were lucky to hold on to their modest wages, and she had exhausted her last lead.

Still seeing no action inside, Nicole walked along the wraparound porch and noticed for the first time a wicker swing near another entrance to the west. Tired, she sat in it and swung slowly, listening to it creak and wondering what stories it could tell if only it—

She heard the clopping and snort of a horse on the other side of the house and she jumped up with a start. Her car was near the main entrance. Whoever was there had to see it and had come looking for her.

Resigned to her fate she flung back her shoulders, thrust out her chest and jutted out her chin. She added a hip-swiveling sashay as she rounded the porch and thought she had captured her character perfectly.

Until one red spiked heel sank and stuck in a crack.

A good-looking cowboy dismounted. She tugged unsuccessfully and nearly broke into hysterical laughter. He stopped short and appraised her, hands on hips. With one mighty yank she heard the crack of her heel as it separated from the sole.

Improvise, she told herself. *Maintain a sense of humor.* She dug into her shallow well of theatrical experience and limped toward him, tempted to try a joke as an ice-breaker. And *ice* definitely described his demeanor.

Losing her nerve, she smiled coyly instead, acting as if this sort of thing happened all the time. He folded his arms against his broad chest and simply stood there, staring at her.

Exasperated, she said, "Well, at least I didn't lose my soul!" It was all she could do to keep the big red smile pasted on her face. *Oh, Lord, help me. I'm dying here!*

Okay, it was corny, but what was wrong with this guy? Most would have found this entrance amusing. And what was he gaping at? Regardless of her getup, she still had to be the most wholesome-looking woman around this place.

Maybe he was testing her under pressure. There had to be some mighty tough hombres frequenting this...this establishment. That had to be it.

She stepped off the porch and thrust out her hand, forcing all the confidence she could muster. "My name is Nicole. I came about—" she hoped he didn't see her gulp "—the job."

He looked at her hand as if measuring the possibility of contamination if he touched it.

"Nicole what?"

"Nicole Bedder."

"Better than what?" he asked all too seriously.

Another time she might have laughed, but this guy had already proven he didn't have a sense of humor. Nonetheless, she played his game. With an exaggerated look over her shoulder, she said, "Better than all the other applicants standing behind me."

Reluctantly he took her hand, gave it a quick shake and said, "Michael Phillips. I own the place." *And what in the hell are you doing on my porch* is what she read in his squinting blue eyes.

"Wait a minute. A *man* owns the—" She'd lost her character a moment, but quickly recovered. Beaming again, her voice sweet enough to cause diabetes, she said, "Hmm. Only fair, I guess. Equal rights and all."

She let go of his long, callused fingers, stepped back and thrust her arms out to her sides. "I'm ready to start right now." *Please! Please!*

He pushed the Stetson higher on his tanned forehead and

stared at her in disbelief. She didn't flinch. But after what seemed to be the most pregnant pause of the decade, she caved and spoke first.

"So...do I get the job?"

Two

When hell freezes over, Michael thought.

"I don't know what job you're applying for, but I need a helper, not a—" he stopped short of *hooker* and let her fill in the blank. He watched the slow batting of her dark lashes and noticed one corner was jutting straight out like a perched insect ready to take flight. He felt a smile tug at one corner of his mouth, but he controlled it. The last thing he wanted to do was encourage this…this spitfire.

"I can help," she said.

He was afraid to ask how. He shook his head. "No, I'm sorry. You're not what I'm looking for." He turned away and started for the door. She was right on his heels.

"How can you tell? You haven't even asked me any questions."

He kept moving, hoping she'd give up and go away, knowing she wouldn't. "For one thing, I need a man." When she didn't respond, he couldn't help but turn. Her brown eyes were round, her mouth open.

"A man? Here?"

"Well…yes." No way could someone so small and frail looking possibly carry a sheet of drywall or a bunch of two-by-fours up a flight of stairs. But then, he was certain that wasn't what she came for.

She closed her mouth and looked defeated, then she took a step closer. "Wait a minute. Isn't that sex discrimination?"

He hiked an eyebrow before giving her his back and walking up the steps to the front door. "Only if you're willing to hire an attorney and take me to court." He knew he had her now. If one thing was certain, her kind wouldn't go looking for a day in court. Not intentionally, anyway.

Michael was halfway through the door when he heard a thud behind him. He turned and found her lying on the brick walk. In two long strides he was beside her and hunkered down.

"Ms. Bedder?" He watched and waited, hoping this was some sort of last-ditch effort to win sympathy. He touched her thin arm. "Ms. Bedder?" He could see her chest moving, though her breathing seemed shallow.

Faking or not, he couldn't just leave her there. He scooped her up in his arms, her remaining shoe falling to the ground, and he was surprised at how light she was. At closer inspection he could see her pale and sallow cheeks, and for a moment he almost felt sorry for her…until he remembered what kind of woman she clearly was.

He carried her to the door and pushed it open with his shoulder, just as her eyes started to flutter open. A quick flash of surprise was followed by an indignant palm against his chest.

"What do you think you're doing? Let me down this instant!"

He had a mind to drop her on her cute little backside, but he didn't. He headed for the sofa and dropped her there instead. The errant eyelash was now pointing straight up and a grin escaped before he could control it.

"What's so funny?"

He pointed to his own eye and watched her squirm. She removed the lash and tucked it in her skirt pocket, leaving her with one long-lashed round eye and one…one beautiful brown one. He wiped the grin off his face and started for the kitchen.

"Where are you going?"

"To get you a glass of water." He stopped and glanced over his shoulder. "Or would you rather have something stronger?"

"I'd rather—" She started to stand, then fell back down.

Michael watched and waited. This woman was definitely not okay. In more ways than one.

She lifted her head off the back of the sofa, removed the remaining eyelash and stared at him for the longest time. It was as though he were seeing a different woman. This one had far less bravado and looked far more vulnerable. Damn. He hoped she wouldn't cry. He hated it when a woman cried.

She lowered her gaze, and again he noticed how frail she looked. Without thinking he asked, "When's the last time you ate?"

Her head popped up, and the original woman reappeared. "Oh, I'm on this fad diet. That's all."

If he'd learned only one thing over the past couple of years, it was to know when a woman was lying. In a flash, images of another woman, another place tugged him back in time. And just as quickly he stuffed them away. Instead, he looked through the front window at the old rattletrap parked in his driveway, then back to this woman's pale face. "Look, I haven't had lunch yet. Would you like to join me?"

Her face brightened and she found the strength to stand.

Great! Now why in the hell had he done that?

The phone rang in the kitchen and he left Ms. Bedder to fend for herself.

Nicole took a deep breath and padded barefoot into the kitchen, where she found Michael leaning on the open refrigerator door, staring blankly inside, a phone propped between his ear and shoulder.

"That's right," he said into the receiver. "The job's still open."

She nudged him aside and proceeded to retrieve lettuce, mayo, lunch meat and pickles from the fridge. Taking it all to a center chopping block, she looked around and found a pantry closet. Inside were bread and potato chips, which she added to her cache on the cutting board.

She pretended not to notice his gaze as he followed her around with his curious blue eyes and carried on his phone call at the same time.

"Do you have your own tools?"

Tools? She almost laughed. Like what? Handcuffs? Leather pants? What kind of tools would a man need for *this* job? She slapped mayo on four slices of bread. Then she decided to make Michael what's-his-name a sandwich, too.

"No, you don't need tools. I was just wondering." He leaned a shoulder into the wall and looked out the bay window to the overgrown garden behind. "Any carpentry or remodeling experience?"

Nicole's knife stilled in her hands. Carpentry? Helper?

She stood frozen over the food, an instant replay of their meeting outside running before her eyes, embarrassment warming her neck and cheeks. All around her were signs of remodeling. And nowhere in sight were the ladies, whose colorful stories she'd heard about in Livingston.

"Sorry. Guess I should have put the location in the ad,"

Michael said behind her. "You're right. It's probably a two-hour drive. Uh-huh. Perfectly understandable. Well, good luck."

Nicole heard him hang up the phone, but she kept her back to him, wondering how she could begin to explain, if she should even try. She cut the sandwiches diagonally and on second thought put three halves on each plate. She added chips and pickles, then carried it all to the cozy table in front of the window.

Before he could join her, one of her sandwich halves had disappeared along with most of her chips. Michael pulled out a chair and sat down, fascinated with the steady rhythm of her hand to mouth to plate and back.

"Some kind of fad diet you got there."

She continued shoveling it in, not meeting his gaze, too intent on the business at hand. When she'd finished the last of it she sat back and closed her eyes, seeming to relish the moment.

Michael picked at his food, his appetite having left him when he realized he'd fallen prey to this hapless creature. It was obvious she was hungry and had been for some time, which meant she was broke, which meant he couldn't send her off if he wanted to.

What bothered him most was that he wasn't sure he wanted to.

There was something more than met the eye here. One moment she was cocky and confident, the next a frightened kitten.

"Aren't you going to eat that?" She was staring at his untouched half sandwich and pickle.

He pushed his plate over and she helped herself.

"Where else have you tried to find work?"

She held up a finger, finished chewing, then said, "You name it." She polished off his dill pickle in three efficient bites, then carried both plates to the sink where she rinsed and stacked them. Then she put everything away and cleaned off the counter, looking as though she'd done this all her life, that this was her home instead of his.

Now she stood in front of him, hands on hips. "Well, I can swing a hammer as well as the next. Paint, wallpaper. Whatever."

"Have you considered getting a job as a cook instead of…instead."

She crossed her arms and glared at him, looking insulted that he might suggest she came for anything other than a carpenter's helper, when he knew full well she hadn't.

"I need a job with room and board." It was more a statement of fact than a request, a certain sound of assurance in her voice telegraphing this was a done deal.

Heaven help him. She was moving in. His gut told him it was true before the words took shape in his head.

He went to the cupboard and started rummaging.

"What are you doing?" she asked, standing close enough that he caught a whiff of her perfume, her words sending a soft puff of warm air skittering over his free arm.

"Looking for the antacid."

"Have you ever tried laughter instead?"

He found the bottle, uncapped it and downed a healthy swig. "What's that supposed to mean?"

She cocked her head in a too-adorable way and said, "You ought to loosen up a little, Michael. Look at that frown on your forehead."

When had they gotten on a first-name basis? And when had her voice changed? It seemed different somehow. Whatever was going on, he knew he'd better take charge of this situation right here and now.

"Look, Nic—Ms. Bedder. You can stay here for a few days and cook…in exchange for room and board." She eyed him for a moment, looking as though she were taking his measure and had suddenly become wary of his intentions, which seemed strange, since she was a woman willing to sell her body to a perfect stranger.

Something just wasn't adding up. But for now it didn't matter. All he wanted to do was make one thing perfectly clear.

"Just a few days, while you look for a job elsewhere. Agreed?"

A slow smile reappeared on her full lips, exposing small, white, perfect teeth. "Agreed."

Nicole raced over the brick walk toward her trusted Chevy until she came to the path's end. There she turned and surveyed the sprawling Victorian, its turrets and furbelows adding grace and beauty to the valley it inhabited. It was a grand old lady, she thought, before turning and tiptoeing over the gravel and popping open her trunk. She could do a lot worse than stay here.

Yet stay she would. And not for a few days, either. Somehow she would convince that—that macho cowboy— that she was the right person for the job. A salaried one, at that. She'd never been afraid of hard work, and after a few good meals her strength would surely return.

Inside her duffel she found comfortable sandals and breathed a sigh of relief as she slipped them onto her hot feet. Throwing the bag over her shoulder, she indulged in a moment of optimism. What if this turned out to be more than a means to an end? Maybe she wouldn't have to take the money and run. It could be the perfect place for—

She was getting ahead of herself. First things first.

When she started back for the house, she saw Michael standing in the doorway, his face lost in shadow. He was waiting for her and watching, not moving a muscle. She tried to recapture her earlier persona as she strode toward him, but she knew some of the cockiness had abandoned her. There was something about fainting that made that role no longer plausible. Something about him carrying her inside that made her feel...

She closed the distance between them and concentrated on the present. He held the door open and she squeezed through the narrow space between him and the door frame. The scent of aftershave floated on a breeze, and she moved quickly, suddenly uneasy.

He took her duffel and said, "Follow me."

They crossed through French doors that led to the west wing, stopping when they reached the first room to the right. He stepped back and with a wave of his arm motioned her in.

"This will be your room."

There was a hint of amusement in his eyes, which confused her. Until she stood in the doorway and looked in. Then she froze, dill pickles revisiting the back of her throat.

"The previous owner had a son. All the other bedrooms are in various degrees of disrepair, so I guess this will have to be it."

In front of her was a young boy's room, decorated in red, white and blue, a twin bed the shape of a race car with an appropriate spread. She took an involuntary step backward, a sharp intake of air sounding loud to her own ears. Her back hit Michael's chest, but he didn't move. Instead he gripped her shoulders and held her firm.

"You're not going to pass out on me again, are you?"

She closed her eyes to what was in front of her and took a cleansing breath. It was only then she realized his hands were still on her. Warm and gentle.

She turned quickly, breaking contact. "N-no, of course not."

He slanted her a disbelieving frown, then turned. "Come on. I'll show you the rest."

* * *

She vaguely remembered Michael showing her the sitting room next to hers and beyond that his own room, but whatever else she'd seen, Nicole would have to explore another time, the image of this room having occupied her thoughts.

She sat gingerly on the race car bed, buried her face in her hands and wondered for what cruel deed she was being punished to be sentenced to this room. Tenaciously, behind the darkness of her fingers, burned bright a dirt-smudged, freckled face.

No! She leaped from the bed and paced to the long, narrow window. She couldn't afford the luxury of self-pity. There was a job to be done, money to earn. People in need.

Compartmentalize, she lectured herself. As often was the case, she imagined her heart as a large warehouse with many private chambers, each storing its own joys and pain, some atrophied with neglect, others—such as the one she accessed now—ripe with worry and longing.

Reluctantly she filed away the pain and surveyed her surroundings with a more objective eye. Someone's little boy had actually lived here. Of that she was certain. But why? What a strange place to raise a child. As with the swing outside, Nicole wished these walls could talk. Or did she? Would she want to store another sad story?

Heavyhearted, she hiked her duffel atop the bed and found places for her meager belongings in the lone dresser—save for one item, a small photo album. She debated between the nightstand drawer and the small desk by the window, finally deciding on the desk. A less likely place for one to look.

She opened the drawer slowly. Inside was a pad of construction paper, all the colors of the rainbow, and her heart was in her throat once again. Quickly she hid her album at the back and closed the drawer. More than anything, she longed to study her precious photos, but the day had been long and dizzying enough. She shed her clothes and headed for the shower, taking her time as the refreshing spray washed away the dust from her hair and limbs, until finally she felt the soothing comfort of optimism return.

Silently she offered up a prayer of thanksgiving. She had found a safe harbor. And with God's help, maybe more.

Of the few calls Michael had received, none had panned out. Building materials loomed at the end of the walk, challenging him to begin alone. He could do it if he had to. And he would. But not today. He looked at his watch: it was time to leave for Taylor's.

He grabbed the keys to his work van, then remembered the bottle of wine chilling in the refrigerator. Backtracking to the kitchen he stopped short when Nicole entered the living room. Her wet hair was pulled back into a simple ponytail, her face scrubbed clean of makeup. If he didn't know better, he'd think someone new had taken her place. Also missing was the attitude, when she crossed the room toward him.

"What time would you like supper?" she asked, almost shyly.

"Uh, well, I'm eating out tonight." And the refrigerator was pretty bare. He should have thought of this before.

"Oh." Suddenly she didn't seem to know where to look.

"I'd say 'help yourself tonight' but there's not much here. Just a few things I picked up on my way through Joeville. The previous owners left staples, baking stuff, but the freezer is empty." He thought a second and came up with an idea. "I could give you some money and you could do some shopping in town."

Her gaze flitted to her car in the drive. "Um, could I wait till tomorrow and use your car?" Then she added hastily, "A lot more bags would fit it yours."

"Not really. The back's full of tools and—"

She lowered her eyes. "I'm not sure I have enough gas."

He watched embarrassment tinge her freshly scrubbed cheeks, and the urge to comfort her flared. The cocky, confident woman of earlier had been much easier to deal with. This one smelled of trouble. The kind he couldn't afford.

"Look, Ms. Bedder—"

"Would you mind calling me Nicole?"

Michael ran a hand through his hair and hid his frustration the best he could. "Nicole...I'm just going to my sister's, the farm next door. Why don't you come along? We'll worry about groceries and gas tomorrow."

"Oh, I couldn't—"

He crossed to her and tugged at her elbow. "I insist. It will be okay." He glanced down at her and met her doelike brown eyes. "Trust me."

Three

Nicole's fears about being the uninvited guest were quickly dispelled when Taylor and Josh welcomed her. She'd heard plenty about the Malone dynasty—the fact that Max Malone was a legendary surgeon and that his three sons, their wives and children all lived on the sprawling miles of ranch and farmland in the shadows of the MoJoe Mountains. It just never occurred to her that the Purple Palace was next door, or that there would be a connection between the owners.

It seemed there was much to be learned about Michael Phillips, a thought that both intrigued and frightened her.

While Josh got Michael a beer, Taylor gave Nicole a quick tour of the house. Had she not known how wealthy the family was, she never would have guessed. There was nothing pretentious about their warm home.

The women were just descending the stairs to the living room when two little ones ran in from the kitchen. The toddler, trying to keep up with her big brother, tripped and fell face first on the bearskin rug in front of the open hearth.

Instinctively, Nicole ran to her, knelt down and righted the child, who seemed startled at seeing a stranger's face so close to hers. When her bottom lip started quivering, Nicole sat cross-legged and pulled the little girl onto her lap.

"My name's Nicole. What's your name?" She tucked a stray blond curl behind the little one's ear, smiled down at her and waited patiently for a reply. Shyly the toddler held up one hand and pulled down all but two fingers.

"You're two years old!" Nicole feigned surprise. "You're so big for two."

A wide smile exposed perfect little new teeth. Her eyes were big and blue like her mother's, and Nicole knew she was hooked, the sweet scent of baby shampoo making it nearly impossible not to squeeze the child closer.

"Em—a—lee," the little girl said, tilting her chin higher.

"Your name is Emily?"

She nodded so hard she nearly toppled over again. Nicole steadied her. "Emily is a beautiful name."

Big brother joined them on the floor. "My name is John. My grandpa's name was John, but he's dead now."

Nicole held back a chuckle. The candor of kids always amazed and delighted her. God, how she missed this. She watched John dash for the bookshelf, and she swallowed hard. Was this a blessing or a curse? Could these little ones help ease the pain? Or would they simply keep the wound open and aching?

John handed her a book and she stopped analyzing. With a smile she watched their eager faces and turned to page one.

Michael couldn't take his eyes off Nicole. Who was this suddenly wholesome-looking woman who played so easily

with children, a woman whose supposed profession seemed
at the opposite spectrum from motherhood? Emily settled
deeper in Nicole's lap, resting her head against Nicole's
chest, while John allowed a gentle arm to slip around his
small shoulders.

Michael leaned into the doorjamb and swigged from a
bottle. Perhaps she wasn't part of the world's oldest profession after all. But then why look for work at the Purple
Palace? He was certain she hadn't come with remodeling
in mind.

A few tendrils of hair had escaped her ponytail and fell
softly down her delicate jawline, thinly veiling the dark
brown eyes that seemed almost too large for her small face.
He remembered how they looked when she stared at him
in surprise as he'd carried her into the house, the weightless
feel of her in his arms, the sense of total vulnerability, both
hers and—

"She's a natural, isn't she?" Taylor whispered.

Michael turned with a start at the sound of his sister's
voice. "Yes. Seems she is."

"I'm surprised at you, little bro." Taylor smiled teas-
ingly.

"Surprised at what?"

"That you'd hire a woman for your helper."

Michael turned Taylor around and herded her into the
kitchen. "Whoa. Wait a minute. I said she came about the
job. I didn't say I was hiring her for it."

Taylor slanted him a doubtful look.

"Really. She's broke and hungry. I said she could cook
and help out, but she'll be gone in a few days."

"Uh-huh. We'll see."

"Yes, you will."

But his sister had to have the last word. "I still can't
believe it—my brother, the cynic, a man who thinks all
women lie as easily as they breathe."

Michael caught her wrist as she started to turn. "Not all women." He winked at her playfully. "I don't think you do."

Taylor's expression grew more serious. "And neither did Mom."

Michael dropped her wrist. "Not now, sis."

"Then when?"

Josh brushed by them and headed for the refrigerator, then stopped abruptly. "Am I interrupting something?"

Michael downed the rest of his beer and set the empty on the counter with a thud. "Just your wife sticking her nose in where it doesn't belong." The words were no sooner out of his mouth than he regretted saying them. With a quick step forward, he kissed her on the nose and tried to make amends. "But what a cute nose it is."

Taylor continued staring at her shoes.

"I'm sorry, sis."

She gave him a bear hug around the waist, but not before he noticed her eyes were bright with moisture. "Me, too."

Josh uncapped another beer behind them and said, "Good. Now that that's settled, when do we eat?"

Josh led everyone in prayer before the procession of platters and bowls started around the table. There was more food here than Nicole had seen in months. Even when she'd had her apartment in Denver and her little day care business, she'd never made this much food for one meal. She simply couldn't afford it.

Yet as delicious as everything looked and smelled, with Michael sitting next to Nicole she only picked at her food, all too aware of his thigh occasionally brushing against hers and the seductive scent of his aftershave. It had been so long since...

"Nicole?"

She looked up with a start at the sound of Michael's husky voice and felt heat creep up her neck to her cheeks.

"I—I'm sorry. I guess I was enjoying this marvelous meal so much I didn't hear the question."

"Taylor asked where you were from," Michael repeated, the vivid blue of his eyes making it difficult for her to concentrate.

"Oh. I'm from De—" she dabbed at her mouth and regrouped "—Delaware."

Michael shot her a dubious look from under his sandy brows, a look she'd seen a number of times today. "Really? How did you end up in Montana?"

She shrugged her shoulders as if to say, Why not Montana? "Always wanted to see the West."

"Me, too." Taylor smiled at her from the far end of the table. "My mother was born out here, but I was raised in Michigan. Came out here for college."

Grateful for the shift in focus, Nicole continued the thread, trying to ignore the distraction next to her. "Is that where you met Josh?"

Josh laughed. "If she knew me from school, she'd never admit it. I guess I had a reputation with the women back then."

"You guess?" Taylor eyed her husband with a coy smile.

Nicole watched the playful banter between the two and saw the look of love on their faces, and pain streaked straight for her heart. Whether it was envy, sadness or simply lost opportunity, she wasn't sure. But it hurt to watch them.

"Actually, we got to know each other when I was Josh's physical therapist. He had this wimpy little shoulder problem he insisted I treat." Taylor winked at her husband, then looked at Nicole. "I used to work with Josh's father. He has a clinic at the ranch up the road."

"Do you miss it? Your therapy work, I mean."

Taylor glanced at her husband before answering the

question. "Funny you should ask. We've been talking about me returning part-time, but we haven't solved the sitter situation yet. Savannah and Jenny have their hands full with their kids and the work they do at the ranch. I couldn't ask—" She stopped talking suddenly and stared at Nicole as if seeing her for the first time, then she looked Michael's way.

"Ouch!" Taylor reached under the table.

John asked, "What's wrong, Mama?"

Taylor glared at Michael with an expression of pain and annoyance. "Nothing, sweetie. Just a little cramp in my leg."

Josh, apparently seeing a problem brewing, steered the conversation back on course. "Sweetheart, tell Nicole how you saved my life."

Taylor waved a dismissive hand before filling her mouth with potatoes and shooting Michael a last angry look.

"Okay. If you don't want to tell it, I will."

Nicole listened with rapt attention as Josh told of his plane crash, paralyzed legs and Taylor's healing hands and heart in the months that followed. And again Nicole felt a tug on her heartstrings. At least some people had found their happily-ever-after.

She chastised herself for her attitude and then counted her blessings as Taylor brought out a chocolate cake and set it in front of her brother to cut. When she returned with a stack of dessert plates and sat down, she touched Michael's arm.

"Tell us about your plans for the Palace, Michael. All you said earlier was that you were expecting some lumber." Michael cut small pieces of cake for the children while he answered, his face warming to the subject. Nicole noticed the lines on his forehead were barely visible now, that the cynicism she'd seen all day had nearly vanished. She couldn't help but wonder about this handsome and complex man sitting across from her. One minute he had a chip on his shoulder; the next he was warm and loving with his family.

"I don't have a lot of free time," Josh said, "but give a holler if you need help."

"What about Billy?" Taylor suggested. "He's sixteen now and really good with his hands. He might have some spare time."

"I'll keep that in mind," Michael said, passing a piece of cake to Josh.

"Gosh, I wish I had the time. You know I love carpentry."

Michael glanced around the comfortable room. "Yes. I remember Dad and I getting the tour of your handiwork just before that Fourth of July party. I think you missed your calling."

Josh smiled, seeming to enjoy the compliment. He ate some cake, then chuckled. "What a party that turned out to be, huh? I had this big plan all worked out to propose to Taylor during the fireworks, then Jenny went into labor. Thank God I could fly her to the hospital before the twins were born. And thank God Dad was in the plane with us. He—"

Nicole saw Michael go pale at the same time as Josh, who fell silent and didn't seem to know where to look. Both men picked up their forks and ate more cake as the silence stretched uncomfortably. Nicole looked from one to the other, trying to puzzle it out. Had something else happened at that party?

Finally Taylor spoke, her voice a little shaky. "And after the remodeling, what do you plan to do with the place?"

Michael took his time answering, looking distracted. "I spent some time researching bed and breakfasts and they seem to be doing well out here. There isn't one for miles around, so I thought the next owner would have a real go at it, especially if a certain family would allow tours of a working ranch, some horseback riding, maybe even a short plane ride over the MoJoes and valley.'' Michael's gaze darted to Josh but it didn't hold.

"The next owner?'' Taylor asked. "I thought you were staying.''

"I am. But could you see me as an innkeeper?'' He laughed at the idea. "I'll be lucky if I have enough money to finish the restoration. As soon as I'm done I'll have to find a job and a place to live.''

"But close by, right?'' Taylor still looked concerned.

Michael pushed out his chair and stood. "Not to worry, sis. That's exactly the plan.'' He reached for her hand, and she stood.

To Nicole's surprise, the men offered to do dishes so the women could play with the children in the yard. She followed Taylor out onto the front porch and sat alongside her on the top step. Together they watched the sun sinking below the MoJoes, and Nicole let out a satisfied sigh. Taylor leaned back on outstretched arms and called out to John to keep an eye on his sister.

"It's awesome, isn't it?'' she asked Nicole. "I hope I never take it for granted.''

"Yes. It is.'' After a moment she added, "Thank you for dinner. It was the best meal I've had in ages.''

Taylor sat up and rested her elbows on her knees, her face reflecting some inner debate. "You're very good with children. You've had experience, haven't you?''

Nicole hesitated only a second. "Yes.'' She wanted to volunteer more, but was afraid where the questions might lead.

"Could you provide references?''

Excitement and hope sent a shiver down her back. Could she? The mothers she'd helped would certainly recommend her, yet she couldn't have mail sent to Joeville without the risk of being tracked down. Then she remembered yesterday and the little post office adjacent to the doughnut shop nearly fifty miles away.

She met Taylor's hopeful smile with one of her own. "It may take a week or two, but yes, I'm sure I can."

"Mind keeping this between us for the time being?"

"No. Not at all."

They watched the children and didn't say much after that, but Nicole knew she had just made her first friend in Joeville. For a moment she thought about asking what had happened to Michael at the party, but she didn't want to pry.

Still, the longer she thought about Taylor's brother, the more she was certain that he had come to this place with baggage of his own. She wasn't the only one with something to hide.

Four

——

Michael dropped a plumb line from the header above the new door frame leading to one of the large upstairs bathrooms, the scent of this morning's bacon lingering in the air, and the image of Nicole lingering in his mind. He'd read the paper and drunk coffee, pretending to ignore her, but when she hadn't been looking, he'd studied her graceful and confident movements around the kitchen. It had been seven years since his mother's death, and until this morning he didn't realize how much he missed the presence of a woman doing what seemed to come natural. It felt good. Damn good.

Damn it. This wasn't smart. In a week or so she'd be gone. He'd be wise to remember that.

He kicked the bottom of the stud so that it aligned with the plumb line, then hunkered down and nailed it in place.

"Refill?"

Over his shoulder Nicole stood with a fresh pot of coffee.

He lifted his mug from the floor, and she filled it, a smile on her face and a fresh floral scent invading his space. Nowhere was there a hint of the woman with the attitude he'd met yesterday. Which was the real Nicole? Or was she a chameleon, someone who could adapt at the drop of a hat? And for what purpose? To ingratiate herself so that she could stay here indefinitely?

"Can I help you with anything?" Her voice sounded sincere enough.

"No, thank you. Breakfast was great." He sipped some of the hot brew and added, "And so is this coffee. Thanks." Damn! Why did he feel so uncomfortable with her standing nearby? He felt awkward and clumsy and so big next to her slight figure.

And what a figure it was, he thought, setting his mug down and turning back to his work. Her knit top, though not snug, could not hide her generous curves. Today's jeans looked even sexier than yesterday's denim skirt. Oh, brother. It had to be his neglected libido speaking. This line of thinking was stupid, stupid, stupid.

"There's a big pot of soup simmering on the stove," she said to his back. "I…I, uh, was thinking maybe I should do a major grocery shopping today…unless you need me for something else."

No, no. Please leave. "You can take the van, if you want. Keys are hanging by the door." He kept hammering at the nail, refusing to meet those big brown eyes.

"Could you check on the soup whenever you're downstairs?"

"Sure."

"It should be boiled-down and thick enough by lunchtime. There's some bread cooling on a rack, too."

"Great."

"Um…I have some personal things to take care of while

I'm out, so I probably won't be back until supper. Is that okay?''

"No problem. Take your time." Please.

"Well, then—"

She was still standing there, her perfume driving him to distraction. What was she waiting for? And then it hit him. Money. She'd need money for groceries.

He stood and retrieved the money clip from his pocket and started counting out twenties. He handed them to her, and she took them shyly, a slight tinge of pink rising in her cheeks. "Do you think this is enough?"

"Oh, plenty, I'm sure." She looked at him soulfully, and this time he couldn't look away. "Thank you, Michael, for everything."

He could feel the heat rising up his neck, and he waved a hand before returning to his work. "See ya later."

He heard her retreating and forced himself not to look over his shoulder, not to notice again the gentle sway of her hips, the just-right curve of her small backside. He blew out a loud breath. It was good she'd be gone all day. He had work to do.

Yes, he lectured himself, downing more coffee. He'd put Nicole out of his mind and get down to business.

He grabbed a handful of nails and dropped them into his tool belt, a little voice at the back of his head reminding him of a more immediate problem—one he'd been avoiding. It was time he sorted things out regarding the Malones. In Michigan it had been easy to think he could deal with the complications of their intertwined families. Here, face-to-face with people he barely knew, it was quite a different matter.

Michael gave up any pretext of working and sat cross-legged on the floor. The subject needed more than a cursory glance, and there was no point putting it off any longer. If he planned to live in Joeville, he'd have to see them sooner or later and make peace. Not that they had ever been at war, he reminded himself. Actually, in the brief time he had met them seven years ago, he liked the whole family.

Even Max. He let out a long sigh, wishing he could sweep away the truth as easily as he did sawdust.

Max.

His father.

How strange that simple thought.

He wasn't the dad that John had been, the man Michael had lived with and worshipped. But nonetheless, Max *was* his father—a fact he hadn't learned until after his return to Michigan—a fact he had denied, or at least refused to dwell on, for all the intervening years.

As long as the good man who raised him was alive, he'd wanted no other father. Even now that his dad was gone, Michael still had trouble thinking of Max in those terms. For all practical purposes, they were strangers. Sure, there would be family gatherings that would force them to be in the same room from time to time, but the family was large and they could get lost in the crowd. They could be civil with each other without the need to go further.

He closed his eyes and pictured his dad working alongside him. All their years together—he'd taken them for granted as if there was no end. Now Michael would give anything to have him here. He would have loved this old place, taken pride in its rebirth. Two peas in a pod, his mom had always said.

The ache in his chest returned as it always did when he thought of his mother. He had always put her right up on that pedestal with his dad. If only she were still alive to answer his questions. Why had she been unfaithful? And why had she deceived them both, taking her lies to the grave with her? He had loved her and trusted her with all of his heart.

Why, why, why?

Frustrated, he stood and picked up his hammer, feeling all the old anger welling up inside him—anger at his mother, anger at Max, anger at Roxanne, the next woman Michael had so unwisely chosen to love, and mostly, anger at himself for his inability to control any of it.

He stalked to the window and gazed down. There, looming at the end of the brick walk, was Nicole's rusted Chevy. He planted his hands on his hips and spoke to it as though it were the woman herself.

"And what am I going to do about you?" He said aloud. Another woman. Another problem. Yet he couldn't just send her packing. She needed work and money first. He remembered Taylor had hinted at a remedy for that, but her solution meant having Nicole stay.

"I'll be damned if I allow that!" He turned and strode back to his work, knowing his words were as hollow as the wind whistling through the open window behind him. He had about as much control over Nicole as everything else. He pushed the tool belt lower on his hips, thoughts of her not wanting to retreat.

Even if—he repeated the word *if* stronger in his head— even *if* she went to work for Taylor, he didn't have to let his guard down with her. She may look fragile and harmless, but underneath, he'd bet anything she was cunning and deceptive.

Ignore the perfume and pretty face, he lectured himself, driving in a nail. Ignore the aroma of the homemade soup wafting up the stairs. He pounded another nail. Ignore the image of her playing sweetly with the children. He drove in two more nails and then threw the hammer on the floor.

As soon as the van was out of sight of the Palace, Nicole pulled off to the side of the road. She opened her oversize denim shoulder bag that sat on the bench beside her. Carefully she extracted the plastic container of hot soup and set it on the floor where it wouldn't spill. Next to it she placed one of the loaves of bread she'd made this morning. Then she opened the newspaper to the pages of coupons and started circling the ones she could use. When she was done, she added the values of each and came to the grand total of just over twelve dollars.

Finally she drove on, her plan firmly in place. First the post office to mail her letters requesting references, then a grocery store where she'd spend as close to twelve dollars as possible.

For once she took advantage of the no-speed-limit law, feeling more confident in Michael's sturdy van. In spite of this, by the time she came to the third and most important part of her day, she had used nearly three hours of the seven she'd allotted herself.

Her heart raced as she wound her way down the narrow dirt road, sending a cloud of dust billowing out behind her. Then she saw it—the hand-carved "Williams" on a wooden sign swinging gently in the wind below a home-made mailbox. She slowed and pulled up the dirt drive alongside the squat log cabin, hoping someone would see her and come rushing out. When no one did, she ran to the front door, knocked once and let herself in. Sprawled out on the floor on his stomach amidst a jungle of logs was her reason for living. He looked over his shoulder at the sound of the door and then scrambled to his feet.

"Mama!"

Nicole scooped the freckled-faced boy into her arms and held him close, inhaling deeply the fresh scent of his tousled hair. "Cody, Cody. I missed you last night."

His little arms tightened around her neck, and she wondered how she could ever say goodbye again, how she could do what she knew she had to do if they were to be safe and together soon.

"I missed you, too, Mama," Cody said as Nicole set him down.

"Pretty soon I won't be able to pick you up. You're getting so heavy, big guy."

He beamed up at her. "That's because I'm seven and a half years old," he said proudly.

Nicole ruffled his sandy hair as Mabel waddled in from the kitchen, her wrinkled face creasing into a big smile at the sight of Nicole. Nicole went to her and kissed her on the cheek. "How's my favorite grandma today?" Mabel's eyes brightened at the compliment. She wasn't really Cody's grandma, but she was the next best thing and the only one he had ever known.

Mabel took Nicole's other hand and led her to the worn sofa, where they sat side by side, Cody snuggling on the other side of his mother. "Tell me what you've been up to, dear. I didn't expect to see you so soon."

"Neither did I." She pulled Cody closer and smiled. "I found a job." It was a stretch, but she knew if Michael didn't hire her, Taylor would. With luck her references would arrive soon.

Mabel covered her mouth, and her eyes grew brighter. She sniffed once and tried to straighten her hunched shoulders. "My prayers have been answered...and so soon! Wait till I tell Walter. He's been so worried about you."

Nicole looked out the windows. "Where is Walter?"

"Deep in the woods, I'm afraid. Berry pickin' or some such. Ya know how he loves his long walks and his critters. Can you stay till he gets back?"

Nicole looked down at Cody under her arm, his eyes pleading with her to say yes, and she thought her heart would break. If only she could take him with her. But she couldn't risk them being spotted together. She'd just have to wait until she'd saved enough money to move on, far away.

"I can stay for a while, but not long. I have to do grocery shopping, and it's more than a two-hour drive to my new place." She watched Cody drop his chin, and she scrambled to change the subject. "Sweetheart, I have some bags in the car. Want to help me carry them in?"

His smile was sweet, and he was trying to act brave, but underneath she worried how all this change was affecting him long-term. She reminded herself she was doing the best she could under the circumstances, but that never seemed to work. She still worried.

Cody helped her carry the bread, soup and twelve dollars worth of groceries inside. She felt guilty about spending Michael's money, but she knew he never would have clipped coupons to save. Besides, when she got money of her own she'd replace it.

Mabel was effusive in her gratitude for the food, and Cody was thrilled with a box of his favorite cereal. It took so little to please them. Watching them find places for their new treasures warmed Nicole's heart and she wished she could have brought more. Next time. Perhaps Wednesdays could be her day off, and she could make this a habit. And maybe next time she could stay longer.

She glanced at the clock over the stove: 2:15. With the drive back and shopping for Michael she'd be lucky to have time to make a quick supper for him.

While Mabel put on a pot of tea, Nicole wrote out the address and phone number of where she could be reached in case of an emergency. She explained that her new employer knew nothing about Cody or her need for secrecy and Mabel completely understood. She and Walter would wait to hear from Nicole unless the unexpected forced them to do otherwise.

Nicole worked on a picture puzzle at the kitchen table with Cody for another twenty minutes, finished her tea and then pulled Cody onto her lap. Lately she'd noticed he'd been avoiding her lap, acting as though he'd outgrown such childish things. Today he came eagerly.

"I have to go, big guy." She nuzzled her nose into his hair, memorizing the smell of it.

He whined, "Just a little longer."

"Not this time, my love. Soon." She hugged him hard and then set him down. He took her hand and walked her to the van as Mabel lingered in the doorway.

"Whose cool van, Mama?"

"The man I work for. He's a carpenter." She knelt down and clasped Cody's narrow shoulders. "You know I wouldn't be leaving you if I didn't absolutely have to, don't you?" She saw tears starting to rim his lower lashes, but he blinked them back bravely.

"I know, Mama." He wiped his nose on the back of his sleeve, then eyed her. "It's all because of that bad man you told me about."

"That's right. Have you looked at his picture lately?"

He shook his head.

"You go find it and look at it with Mabel after I leave. You have to remember what he looks like so you can hide if you ever see him, remember?" She hated to say anything that might frighten him, but he had to know.

"I remember what car," he said, showing a hint of his gap-toothed smile. "A Cadillac. A big Cadillac." He stretched out his arms as far as they could reach.

Nicole poked him in the tummy. "You and your cars." She kissed him quickly on the cheek, afraid to take a moment longer. She opened the van door, hopped up on the seat and slammed it shut. Through the open window she said, "See ya later, alligator," and forced a big smile.

Cody ran alongside the van and called back, "After while, crocodile."

She watched and waved at him in her rearview mirror

until the first bend in the road, then she let the first tears spill.

Nicole sped up the gravel road to the Palace, worried about the fact that it was nearly six o'clock and that Michael might think she wasn't holding up her end of the bargain. He had asked so little of her in exchange for food and shelter. This wasn't exactly the way to start, the way to prove he needed her and increase her chances to stay.

She no sooner cut the engine and opened the door than he strode out, freshly showered and changed into a clean white T-shirt, one that accented his muscles and deep tan. He sauntered closer and she could see that the ends of his brown hair that hung recklessly down his neck were still wet. Suddenly she realized he was watching her watching him, and she averted her eyes.

"Did you clean out the place?" he asked as she moved to the rear of the van and opened the doors. She listened for reproach in his voice, but didn't hear any.

"Not quite," she said, picking up a bag in each arm and heading for the house. "Sorry I'm so late. It won't happen again." It was easier talking to him when she didn't have to look at him. She never knew quite what she'd find when she did. Sometimes he was studying her, making her feel naked. Others he was accusing her, making her feel deceptive, which of course she was. She had no choice. But mostly what she saw was a very handsome and basically good man.

And that's what bothered her most.

She heard the rustle of bags behind her and glanced back. "You don't have to do that. I can manage."

"I've got nothing better to do. I'm done for the day."

"You must be starved." He elbowed open the screen door and held it for her, forcing her close to him. She could smell his soap and felt his warm breath on her shoulder as she passed.

"Had another bowl of that great soup a while ago, so I'm fine."

They made three more trips to the van and back before starting the process of putting everything away.

Now who was *this* Michael, Nicole wondered, watching him out of the corner of her eye. He seemed friendly and relaxed. It made her nervous. For some reason she found dealing with his cynicism easier.

"Jenny brought over a meat loaf and scalloped potatoes. They're in the oven staying warm...so you don't have to worry about dinner tonight."

He'd waited for her? Why?

"Jenny is Josh's sister-in-law. The one who had twins when I was here last time. A couple of little girls. They'll be seven soon."

She turned away, busying herself with another bag, not wanting him to see the pain on her face. Cody was seven. No! She couldn't allow herself to think about him now. Later she would look at her album in the privacy of her room. "That must have been some night...I mean when Josh flew her to the hospital. Good thing his dad is a doctor and was along—" She turned back to place the last of the groceries into the refrigerator just in time to catch the same expression on his face that she'd seen last night...when Max's name was mentioned.

"Would you like a glass of wine? There's a bottle in there chilling."

The change of subject was so abrupt that it caught her off guard, and she heard herself saying, "That would be nice" before she could weigh the wisdom of her decision.

Michael uncorked the bottle and poured while she set the table, took the dinner from the oven and placed the pottery dishes atop trivets on the table. When they were both seated at the small round oak table, Michael raised his glass to her and she lifted her wine tentatively. He clinked her glass and said, ''Cheers.''

''Cheers,'' she said back, unable to hold his intense gaze. What was this all about? She didn't have to wait long to find out.

''So, Nicole,'' he said, setting his glass down, ''don't you think it's time you told me the truth?''

Five

Nicole nearly choked on her wine. "Wh-what do you mean?"

He gave her a sideways look. "You know very well what I mean—that whole act you put on when you applied for the job."

She twisted the glass in her hands, not knowing where to start or how to answer his question without raising more.

"You've never worked at a place like the Purple Palace, have you?"

She glanced up, then back at her hands, finally shaking her head slowly from side to side.

"Then why those silly red spikes and that...that—" he waved his hand near her head "—pile of hair?"

Even though she felt foolish under his close scrutiny, at least these questions she could answer truthfully. "I...I just wanted to fit in. I didn't want to look too straight. You know—someone who might easily be offended at what went on here—or what I thought went on here.'' She could imagine how different she must have looked then compared to now. Out of the corner of her eye she could see Michael shaking his head.

And then he laughed, loud and long. Once he got his composure, he asked, ''What on earth would a helper do at a bordello?'' He took a sip of wine, swallowed quickly and then laughed again.

Nicole couldn't keep a straight face any longer. Her charade had to have seemed comical, but watching Michael break up like this was even funnier. She never could watch someone laugh without laughing herself. And the harder she laughed the louder Michael got.

''See?'' she said finally, wiggling a finger at his unlined forehead and trying to catch her breath.

''See what?''

''That laughter's better than antacids?''

He kept laughing and so did she. At one point she thought she had it under control until she remembered her ideas of what a helper might actually do. It didn't help that Michael was still laughing and wiping his eyes.

Finally her side began to hurt and she got the hiccups. She took a deep breath and held her nose, but the only purpose that served was to amuse Michael further. Eventually he got up and walked behind her, first raising her arms above her head, then pounding her between the shoulder blades.

''I'm not choking,'' she said between giggles. ''It's just hiccups.''

His hand eased up on her back and started rubbing in slow, circular movements. ''Sorry. You're right.''

She could smell his soap again and the scent of something far more dangerous—a man with something more than help on his mind. Whether she stiffened and he felt it or he checked his own reaction, she wasn't sure. But suddenly the room was quiet except for a chorus of crickets and the distant plaintive cry of an animal in the wild.

Michael sat down again and they both reached for their wine at the same time, providing them with an excuse not to speak.

Something was beginning that frightened her. Not just the questions—and there would surely be more—but the way she caught him looking at her from time to time. And worse, the way she was starting to view him.

On the Wednesday trek to town two weeks later, Nicole received the reference letters she'd been waiting for. She clutched them to her chest and closed her eyes, praying they would be enough to get her the job. It would only be part-time and probably not much money, but it was a start. She thought of Jenny's twins and wondered if they might be added to the mix. Then there was another sister-in-law's two children, she remembered. Six would make a nice-size group and give the cousins more time together.

It was a plan, she decided as she headed north for the Williams's house and Cody. Not for the first time she entertained the possibility of making Joeville her home. It was fairly isolated. Could she and Cody live at the Palace without being found? Was there *any* place that was safe? And what would Michael think when he learned that she had a son?

As buoyed as she'd been with the letters and her visit with Cody, these questions distracted her all afternoon and through a fitful night's sleep. After breakfast the next morning Nicole stripped both their beds, washed the sheets and then took her basket to the backyard.

It was mid-May and the sun shone bright in the big Montana sky. She flung the first sheet over the line and spread it evenly, extracting clothespins from her mouth as she moved along. It was a simple task, but one she had missed while living at her Denver apartment with its basement coin-operated machines. She remembered an earlier time, at home with her parents, the snap of linens and the crisp, fresh scent of her bed later. Life had been so simple then.

Before Robert. Not Bob. Robert. He had said Robert commanded more respect, authority. That should have been her first clue, but she had been so enamored by his dark good looks and brooding ways that she saw nothing of the danger lurking ahead. He must have sensed her own restlessness, knowing that when her parents forbade her to see him anymore, it would be all he needed to suck her deeper into his twisted life.

Nicole hung the last sheet and walked back inside. At least Cody had come from that time. For that she would be eternally grateful. Michael called from the porch and she doubled back.

"Mind holding the door a sec?" he asked.

Nicole stepped out of the way while Michael passed her, carrying a sheet of drywall. "Want me to help?" she asked as he headed for the stairs.

He grunted and shifted his load. "No, I got it."

She watched his arm muscles flex and caught herself checking the tight fit of his jeans as he ascended the stairs. And then a sudden wave of sadness passed over her and she looked away.

What a helper she'd turned out to be. She knew he appreciated good meals and a clean house, but that wasn't what he'd asked for or what he needed most. How much longer could she stay here without making herself more useful? The phone rang in the kitchen and she went to answer it.

"Nicole!" The sound of Taylor's voice was a welcome distraction. Nicole had been wondering how to pass the reference letters to Taylor discreetly, and now her new friend provided the solution. They were invited for supper tonight, if they didn't have plans.

Nicole laughed. "I never have plans, but I'll have to get Michael and ask him." She started to put the phone down.

"Wait," Taylor said urgently. "I wanted to ask you if you were still interested in baby-sitting."

"Oh, yes. Very much so. I got my letters yesterday."

"And I bet they rave about you."

Embarrassed, she simply said, "They gave phone numbers if you want to interview them."

"Bring the letters tonight and we'll talk more."

"I really appreciate this, but I'm not sure Michael—"

"Oh, pooh. Let me worry about little brother. He might sound tough, but in case you haven't noticed, he's just an old softy."

She had noticed. While Taylor ran through the menu for tonight Nicole half listened, her thoughts drifting to the sometimes-gruff, but always-gentle man upstairs. More than once she'd caught him unawares as he stooped in the fields of wildflowers near the house for a closer view.

Taylor fell silent and Nicole said, "I'll go get him. Hang on." Between swings of his hammer she called up to him and he raced down the steps, wiping his brow with his sleeve as he took the phone.

"Hi, sis. What's up?"

Nicole wandered into the next room, yet she couldn't help but hear him clearly.

"Sounds great. What time?"

There was a pause and then she heard the change in his voice. At first she thought it was a reaction to her tagging along, but then it became clear it was something else.

"What kind of a surprise, Taylor? This doesn't involve Max, does it?"

Again Nicole wondered what could have happened between the two men. From all she had heard for miles around, Max Malone was a well-liked and respected man. She'd never heard one bad thing about him.

"Okay," Michael said behind her. "If you're certain." Then his tone lightened. "Now you've got me curious. Aren't you going to give me a clue? Thought so. All right then. See ya at six."

At 5:45 Michael waited outside for Nicole, enjoying the late-afternoon breeze rippling through the wildflowers as far as the eye could see. A rare moment of serenity settled over him. Gone were the rush-hour traffic jams and dense push of humanity racing for who knew where. This had been a good decision, he thought, letting his gaze travel back to the house.

From the front door stepped Nicole holding a pie with both hands, an image of complete femininity and grace. Her long, flowing blue skirt caught in the wind and clung to her thighs. Her hair, more silky brown than blonde these days, fell in a neat braid down her back, the blue ribbon tied at the end trailing over her white gauzy blouse.

If she knew he was gaping at her she didn't show it. She strode around the front of the van and settled herself into the passenger seat without a word, a Mona Lisa smile giving her the look of a woman content with the world…one with private thoughts she held close.

Michael knew about private thoughts, but seldom did they bring contentment. He grabbed the steering wheel and hauled himself up.

They drove the two-track path to the farm with the windows down, the sweet smell of sage and fertile earth whipping in around them mixing with the scent of warm apples and cinnamon from the pie on Nicole's lap. He liked the fact that she remained silent. He hadn't met many women who didn't feel the need to fill every quiet moment with conversation. In fact, there was much to like about this small woman beside him.

And that was what scared him.

It had been easier to keep his distance when he'd thought she might be a hooker. Now he didn't know quite what to think. She was still holding something back; he could see it in her eyes now and then. Yet she didn't owe him her life's story, just as he didn't owe her his.

The van crested the ridge and he saw the farmhouse ahead. He sat taller in his seat and reminded himself that Nicole would be leaving soon. That was the agreement. Surely with her personality and skills she'd find something any day now. He'd seen her reading the daily paper, and on Wednesdays she would leave early and barely make it back in time for dinner. That had to be when she went for interviews. What else would keep her so busy?

He pulled up the long drive to Taylor and Josh's, and a dour feeling pressed against his sternum. Without realizing it he had gotten used to Nicole's presence. He would miss her when she left.

He cut the engine just as John ran out to greet him, his blond hair slicked back, his clean little face beaming with excitement. He grabbed Michael's hand and started tugging him toward the front door.

"Come on, Uncle Mike. We got a surprise."

Michael looked over his shoulder at Nicole who trailed behind him, shrugging her shoulders and smiling sweetly. They traipsed up the stairs to the porch and Michael felt his own excitement rising. What did his sister have up her sleeve now?

Taylor held the door while the threesome passed, a flurry of greetings diverting Michael's attention for only a moment.

And then he saw her. The silhouette of a woman in front of the dining room window, her straight hair turned neatly under just above her narrow shoulders. His breath hitched in his throat and he stood rigid. Then the woman turned slowly and started moving toward him, her arms held wide. As she moved away from the bright backlight of the window, her features came into focus and he started breathing again.

"My goodness, Michael, you look like you've seen a ghost."

Michael returned the woman's embrace, not letting on his true thoughts. "Aunt Molly!" She had her sister's frame and hair, but that was where the resemblance stopped. "What a great surprise," he said, holding her at arm's length and seeing just a hint of his mother's face.

"I told ya, Uncle Mike."

Molly pulled back and looked Michael up and down, a sheen settling over her hazel eyes. "It's been so long…too long."

"Yes, it has, Aunt Molly."

"Molly. Just Molly…please. The other makes me feel too old." She looked past Michael and asked, "Aren't you going to introduce me to your young lady?"

He wanted to explain she wasn't his young lady, but Nicole handed the pie to Taylor and stepped forward, her hand already extended.

"I'm Nicole. Nice to meet you, Molly."

"Nice to meet you, Nicole." Molly took Nicole's hand and winked at Michael, who rolled his eyes.

Josh carried a platter of steaks from the kitchen and set it down on the table. "Sorry. They got done quicker than I planned." Everyone found a seat around the table, and conversation flowed freely for the next hour.

Later John took his sister outside to play, and the adults lingered over coffee and Nicole's apple pie.

"How long are you here for?" Michael asked.

Molly gazed out the window, her smile fading. "I'm not sure, Michael. I'm just taking one day at a time."

There was definitely a problem, but Michael didn't feel comfortable probing. He studied her more carefully. She didn't look sick, and by the looks of the new Buick in the driveway, she didn't seem hurting for money.

"Your uncle—" she started, then stopped. "We got divorced last year." The faint smile didn't quite reach her eyes. "I've been doing some traveling, trying to get used to—" She drank a sip of coffee and didn't finish.

The children ran in from outside, the screen door banging behind them. Emily climbed up on her mother's lap while John washed his hands and returned to the table for a piece of pie.

Josh picked up the coffeepot from the sideboard and refilled Molly's cup. "Well, you've come to the right place, Molly. And you can stay as long as you'd like...if you don't mind the sofa bed in the living room."

Michael wished the Palace's remodeling was further along, but the only two bedrooms in good shape were his and Nicole's.

"You can sleep in my bed, Aunt Molly. I like sleepin' on the couch," John said.

"Thank you, dear. That's very nice of you."

He glowed, taking a big forkful of pie. Then his eyes grew round with excitement. "I know! Why don't we have a big party so Aunt Molly can meet everybody...all my cousins and aunts and uncles, Hannah—" He tapped his chin, concentration pinching his fair brows. "Somebody else. Oh! I remember. Grandpa Max." John looked around, seeming to notice the silence that developed around him. "Aunt Molly?"

"Yes, dear?"

"You like parties, don't you?"

"Of course, but—"

"Everybody's real friendly. They'll be real nice to you. Honest."

Michael couldn't remain silent another moment. This was his problem—this thing with Max. The whole family shouldn't suffer.

"I think a party sounds like a great idea, don't you, sis?"

Taylor stared at him, nonplussed. He glanced at Josh and saw a relieved drop in his brother-in-law's shoulders.

"Good. Then it's settled." Michael ushered Molly over to the sofa and she sat down. "We can work out the details later." He turned and saw Nicole hanging back in the doorway, a warm smile directed straight at him. She couldn't know what he had just done, but somehow she'd sensed it was important and she was telegraphing her approval. He held her gaze and wondered if he would ever tell her.

She turned slowly and walked away, looking as though she were weighing thoughts of her own. He heard the door open and close and her light footfalls on the porch. He glanced over his shoulder and saw her walking from the house as Taylor and the children followed.

His heart warmed at the ease with which the women had connected, how the little ones trailing along seemed so eager for Nicole's company. He may regret this in the morning, but he knew what he was hoping. He hoped his sister would offer Nicole a job. He hoped she would stay. He hoped—

No. He'd better leave it at that.

"Are you sure you don't mind?" Nicole couldn't believe her good fortune. Not only had Taylor offered her the job, but now Michael was giving his blessing. "It would mean I'd still be staying here, you know? They don't have an extra room for me."

"I know," Michael said.

The steady squeak of the wicker swing beneath them was

beginning to relax her. Another hurdle had been cleared. At last she let out a long sigh.

"I'll have to start paying rent, of course."

"Don't you plan to cook and help around here anymore?"

"Well, sure. I'll only be baby-sitting Tuesdays and Thursdays…at least for now. I can prepare things ahead those days like I do Wednesdays."

"Then for now you're still earning your keep. Nothing has changed."

Oh, yes, it has. And she could feel it. Not just in his kind offer to keep her on, but the way he let his thigh rest against hers, the way he carefully draped his arm across the back of the swing, brushing her back and shoulders ever so lightly, like a teenager at a movie, trying and failing to be subtle.

The longer they sat there, staring out at the night and its lonely sounds, the more she longed to lean into him, to feel his arm tighten around her. All these years she had pretended not to miss the nearness of a man, convincing herself she didn't dare risk another mistake. Yet sitting beside her was a man far different from the only one she had given herself to. Maybe…

A gentle breeze stirred the grass and drifted lazily over the porch, and she shivered.

"Cold?" Michael asked, not looking at her, trying to sound casual, she noticed.

She smiled straight ahead. "A little."

His arm pulled her closer and she closed her eyes, letting her head rest under his chin and against his broad chest as she curled her feet under her. Michael kept the swing moving ever so slightly, his hand trailing gently up and down her arm. The warmth of him spread through her, the motion lulling her into a place she wanted to go. This was the way it was supposed to be between a man and woman, she thought, wishing the swing would never stop, that they could sit here like this forever.

But then the swing did stop, and she lifted her head. He cupped her chin gently and turned her face toward his. His eyes reflected moonlight and passion as they zeroed in on her mouth. She licked her lips in anticipation, and he accepted the invitation.

The kiss was warm but light, never demanding more. He was the first to end it, kissing the tip of her nose just as softly. He pulled her closer and she could feel his warm breath near her ear.

"This could get complicated, you know."

Her heart was pounding so fast she couldn't speak. It wasn't a question that needed an answer. But yes, this did complicate things. How could she care about this man and not tell him everything? Yet at this very moment logic wasn't in control.

She waited, with his arms wrapped around her, hoping for another kiss. But it didn't come.

Later, lying in her bed, she thought it was just as well. But the feel of him lingered, and she ran her fingertips over her lips, wondering what it would be like to share Michael's bed.

A bathroom and small parlor separated her room from his, but she lay very still, hoping to hear evidence that he was moving about. Once she thought she heard the squeak of a door and then nothing. She waited and waited for more, but after a while she felt herself sinking deeper into the mattress until finally sleep stole the night.

Michael couldn't sleep. He slipped out the porch door as quietly as he could, trying not to disturb Nicole, and then he sat back down on the swing.

He looked out at the miles of flat land that stretched to the foothills and mountains beyond. This is what he'd come to Montana for—this beautiful land, this grand old lady of a house close to his sister and her family.

And to escape the home of his youth. The home where his mother had lied to him all of his life. The home where he'd taken Roxanne for nearly two years—the woman he thought he'd marry and spend his life with.

The woman who cheated on him the last few months of their relationship and then lied to him time and again until he learned the truth about a year ago.

Now, all this time later and miles away, he wondered if it hadn't been his ego that had been damaged more than his heart. Roxanne never would have moved here. She was more comfortable in a suit and corporate setting, something he'd accepted at the time.

He slouched in the swing, hiked a boot over one knee and looked straight up at the endless sky. Yes, this was where he belonged. This was meant to be.

He closed his eyes, and Nicole's image pushed forward, thoughts of her never far away now. She wasn't anything like Roxanne. He knew that intellectually. But emotionally could he trust himself to care again? Could he trust Nicole?

Then he remembered the feel of her lips on his and wondered if his questions were a day late and a dollar short. He slapped his palms against his knees and pushed off the swing.

Things had seemed so simple when he'd first decided to move here. He tried to muster up a little anger as he let himself back inside, but the sight of her closed door and the knowledge of the woman in the room wouldn't allow it.

Six

The cloudless Memorial Day weekend carried through to Monday, the temperature already in the eighties as Nicole prepared to leave for the party just before noon. She'd been looking forward to this day, to spending time with other people. All this one-on-one with Michael was making her edgy.

It had been nearly a week since he'd first kissed her, and it hadn't happened again. He was nice to her, but that was it. Still, for some reason, she didn't think what was bothering him had to do with her. She wished he would tell her what was wrong, but until he was ready she had no choice but to be patient. Yet whenever she remembered the feel of his warm lips on hers—which was often—patience was nowhere to be found.

She heaved a frustrated sigh and returned her attention to boxing the raspberry tarts she'd made earlier this morning. As she covered them with foil, she couldn't help but think of Cody. The tarts were his favorite. If only he could be here.

Soon, little one. Hopefully, soon.

She removed a tub of whipped topping from the refrigerator and wrapped it, letting her thoughts drift to the day ahead. Today she would meet the rest of the Malones. She'd heard so much about Jenny and Savannah from Taylor that she felt as though she knew them already.

Michael sauntered into the kitchen and leaned on the counter beside her. He wore a light blue knit shirt that made the blue of his eyes even more vivid. An all-consuming heat surged through her and she had to look away.

"Ready?" he asked, sounding a bit nervous.

She pretended not to notice his mood. "Yep."

His long fingers gingerly lifted the food, and the heat coursing through her intensified. His hands were strong yet gentle and it didn't take a quantum leap for her to imagine how they would feel...

She took a deep breath and followed him outside as he carried the food to the van. Once she was buckled into her seat he set the tarts and topping on her lap, his fingers brushing her thighs, and she suppressed a groan.

Michael eased behind the wheel and drove to the farm without speaking, but the silence wasn't as comfortable as other times. For a second she wondered if he had read her thoughts or had picked up on her unintentional body language. Or was he so distracted with his problem that her growing desire had totally eluded him? She guessed the latter.

As far as she knew, Michael had yet to see Max since moving here. Today he would. She wondered if this was the problem. Maybe today she would learn why Max was such an issue for him.

And maybe today she could rein in her emotions and think of something else besides lusting after her boss.

Maybe.

* * *

One by one the Malones streamed into Taylor and Josh's front yard, each bearing dishes of food or lawn chairs. Games were played, children and adults alike, voices and laughter carrying across the fields throughout the day.

The afternoon turned to dusk with Nicole watching Michael from afar. All day he had seemed somewhat detached. Just once did she see him with Max, and that was when Max shook Michael's hand when he arrived.

In spite of Michael's mood, Nicole was having a good time. Taylor's sisters-in-law were as warm and fun as promised, and more often than not she found herself in their company, laughing with them and enjoying their precious little ones. Occasionally she caught herself comparing Michael to the Malone men and quite biasedly telling herself she lived with the hunkiest of the hunks. But then she would remind herself that she didn't truly "live" with Michael...not in the way that she would like to—a thought that would unnerve her and drive her back to visiting with the women.

As the day drew toward an end, while cleaning up the kitchen with the others and putting away leftovers, Jenny let out a hoot and wagged her finger toward the backyard.

"Look at that!" she said, starting to laugh. "Bet I know what that's all about." The women followed Jenny's gaze to Hannah, the Malone housekeeper, who was bending Molly's ear and waving in the direction of the ranch. "That crusty old lady's at it again," Jenny said, shaking her head.

Savannah flung her dish cloth over her shoulder and went to the window. "What do you mean?"

Jenny hooked Savannah's arm and nodded to the pair outside. "I saw the wheels turning in Hannah's head as soon as she heard Molly was divorced and would have to sleep on the couch while she was here.''

"Ahh, yes.'' Savannah smiled. "The matchmaker at work.''

"Afraid so,'' Jenny agreed. "How many times has she tried to get Max to one of her church socials?'' They looked at each other and laughed before returning to their work. To Nicole, she added, "That Hannah. She won't be happy until all her men have a mate. Poor Molly doesn't stand a chance.''

Nicole glanced at Taylor who gave her a sly wink. Nicole lowered her eyes, feeling her cheeks warm at the thought of Hannah working on her and Michael someday.

Taylor turned her attention back to the other women. "One week in the Lucky Room and Molly's a goner.''

Nicole watched the three women as they laughed again and shared a private joke. Then one by one they told their stories of time spent in the special room above the kitchen at the ranch. Nicole laughed along with the others, but she couldn't help but feel a pang of envy. They were all so settled and happy with their little families…with husbands they loved who loved them. After Robert, she didn't think she would ever again entertain the idea—

Max strolled into the room, and she filed her personal thoughts away.

"What's all this fun I hear?'' he asked, a warm smile on his face.

Jenny was first to recover. "Just girl talk, Max. Just girl talk.''

He slanted her a suspicious look and smiled as he glanced around her to the backyard where Hannah was still talking with Molly. "Uh-huh. I see.'' He leaned on the doorjamb, seeming in no hurry to leave.

As Nicole studied his handsome, tanned face, the gray at his temples adding a layer of sophistication and charm, he crossed to her and laid a warm hand on her shoulder. "I hear I have you to thank for getting my favorite physical therapist back."

His eyes were kind, and she found herself wondering again how Michael could possibly have a problem with this man. "There's no need to thank me, Dr. Malone. I'm looking forward to caring for the children."

"Max, please."

She met his smile with one of her own, noticing for the first time a certain sadness around his eyes, the kind born of years of pain or loneliness. She couldn't be sure which. But all of a sudden she hoped the girls were right, that Molly might add some sunshine to this man's life.

Jenny left the window and crossed over to Nicole. "You know, if you think you could handle a couple more, I wouldn't mind having a break now and then."

She had met the little dark-haired twins earlier and found them adorable. "I'd love to. Anytime."

Taylor put the last of the leftovers into the refrigerator and said, "We're starting with Tuesdays and Thursdays if you want to join in now."

Savannah moved closer. "Hey! What about Chris? He'd love to spend more time with his cousins. His little sister, Haley, too. She's been clinging lately. Would do her some good to get away from me now and then."

"The more the merrier," Nicole said, trying not to show her excitement. She'd missed her little day care business in Denver, but just as important, she could hear the ching of the cash register. The faster the dollars came in, the sooner she'd be reunited with Cody. Another little voice added, *And the sooner you'll be able to move on,* but she ignored it.

Savannah frowned suddenly, looking as though she'd thought of a problem. She tapped her fingers on the counter a moment before speaking. "Mornings are so hectic at the ranch…what with breakfast, getting the men out the door and early patients in the clinic. Driving the children over here and back twice a day would take a chunk out of the schedule. Taylor, what would you think about bringing Emily and John with you when you come to work?''

Taylor shrugged. ''Doesn't matter to me where we do it. Will it bother Hannah to have so much commotion?''

''Are you kidding?'' Jenny said. ''Since Savannah and I've taken over most of the household chores, she's bored out of her gourd. She'll probably be making them cookies and driving Nicole crazy.''

Nicole shook her head. ''Can't have too many adults loving children. I'm sure we'll get along just fine.''

''Good,'' Taylor said. ''Then it's settled. Starting tomorrow morning.''

Michael called to Taylor from under the kitchen window, ''Got any beer in there?''

''Sure. But don't expect me to wait on you.'' She turned and winked at the women as she pulled a bottle from the refrigerator.

Michael came through the back door with a smile. Until he saw Max across the room. And then he froze.

Nicole watched and felt the tension as Taylor handed Michael the bottle. He took it from her, twisted off the cap and took a long draw. Then he turned his back to everyone and stared silently out the window.

''Well,'' Jenny said after an awkward moment. ''Speaking of kids, I think it's time I get mine home and into the tub. Great party, Taylor. See ya in the morning.''

''Right,'' Savannah added, kissing Taylor on the cheek. ''Thanks for everything, sweetie. Bye, Nicole.'' She paused and looked at Michael's back. ''Good seeing you again, Michael.''

He half turned. ''You, too.''

Nicole shifted her gaze from Max to Michael, holding

her breath, hoping something good would come of this unexpected encounter. Maybe if she and Taylor just slipped
from the room—

"Ready to go, Nicole?" Michael asked, swigging beer,
his back still to Max.

She glanced at Taylor, who was folding a towel, her eyes
cast down and looking as though she might cry.

"Anytime you are," Nicole said, feeling sad herself and
frustrated with her lack of information. If only she understood the problem.

"I'm ready now." He thunked the bottle down on the
counter and said, "Thanks, sis." And then he left the way
he came without so much as a backward glance at Max.

Nicole saw the pain on Max's face. It was nearly palpable, so much so that it was all she could do not to go to
him and put her arms around him. But Michael was waiting, so she simply thanked Taylor for a lovely day, directed
a gentle goodbye to Max and left.

It was nearly eleven when Nicole gave up trying to sleep.
She tightened the belt of her robe and stepped tentatively
out onto the porch, not sure what mood she would find
Michael in, but feeling drawn to him nonetheless. If only
he would talk to her about what was eating him.

"Mind if I join you?"

He patted the space next to him and, to her relief, flashed
a warm smile over his shoulder. "Did you have a good
time at the party?"

Until the end, yes, but she didn't say that. Instead she
told him about her growing day care business and that it
had been moved to the ranch. She glanced out of the corner
of her eye to see how he felt about her working at Max's,
but he gave nothing away.

"So you'll have all of them except Billy."

"Yes." She pictured the lanky young man, so much

older than the others. "It must have been lonely for him…I mean until the rest of the children came along."

"I'm sure it was. Especially living at a place like this."

"Here? I don't understand."

Michael explained how Billy was the son of the now-deceased madam of the Purple Palace, the son whose bed she now slept in. He told her how Ryder befriended the little one, adopting him when his mother died of leukemia when he was only seven. Nicole listened as the story unfolded, imagining the pain that young Billy must have endured and glad that Michael was sharing *something* with her, even if it wasn't what she had hoped to learn. Out of the corner of her eye she watched his hands resting in his lap. She longed to reach out and touch them, to feel his fingers laced in hers, the warmth of his skin on hers. And again an inner fire burned as she held herself in check.

When Michael finished, she braved another look and asked, "Does he ever see his real father?"

Michael's jaw muscles tightened. "Ryder *is* his real father. He's the one who took him in, who cared for him as his own."

"Y-yes. I agree." The intensity in Michael's voice startled her, yet she knew he was right. After all, she would never call Robert her son's real father simply because of his thirty-second contribution.

"So what did you think of the rest of the Malone clan?" he asked, diverting the conversation and sounding as though he thought he might have been too brusque.

"I liked them. Very much." She'd always wished she'd had brothers and sisters and she told Michael so.

"What about your parents?"

It was an innocent enough question, yet she felt her back stiffen.

"Are they still alive?"

There was no way she could dodge the bullet. "I...I assume so."

"Assume?"

"I haven't seen them since I was eighteen." She put her bare feet on the edge of the swing and pulled her knees to her chest, wrapping her arms around her legs. Michael stopped the swing and let his hand trail down her back. When she shivered he slid closer and pressed himself next to her, his hand slipping around her shoulder. It was what she had hoped he would do, but now that he had, she found it difficult to concentrate.

She had come out here hoping to learn something about his problem with Max and to possibly help him sort things out. Instead Michael had turned the tables and was probing into her troubled past. She had already said more than she should have. She didn't want to lie to him, yet the truth of the matter was her parents hadn't approved of Robert. They had made it perfectly clear that if she got in trouble because of "that man," she shouldn't come crying to them. And she didn't.

How could she tell Michael any of this without having to tell him the rest? And how could she focus on anything when her fantasies were running wild with each gentle stroke of his fingers down her arm?

Finally she found her voice. "Do you mind if we change the subject?"

He exhaled loudly and sounded disappointed. "Okay. What would you like to talk about?"

She tucked her legs under her and gazed up at the sky, relieved that he let the subject drop and trying her damnedest not to dwell on his touch. "Oh, let's see...how about the house?"

"Ahh...the house." He gave her arm a tight squeeze before withdrawing his and leaning forward, elbows on knees. "A nice safe subject for both of us." He looked over his shoulder, his expression saying he was just as pleased to steer clear of personal matters as she was. "What about the house?"

Instantly she missed the warmth of his body, but at least it was easier to think. "Have you ever thought of possibly keeping it when you're finished?"

He barked out a laugh. "Taylor asked me the same thing." He shook his head. "Construction is one thing, but being an innkeeper is quite another. I like people, don't get me wrong. Wouldn't mind the meet and greet part at all. But I'd have to hire someone to cook and clean. By the time I paid for that, I don't know if I'd net enough to make ends meet."

But what if he didn't have to pay for those things? The idea that popped into her head scared the wits out of her. She sat very still, her overactive imagination stoked again.

"Although giving her up to someone else is going to be hard."

She mentally shook herself. She felt so out of control. Where was the old confident and focused Nicole? *The house. Talk about the house.*

"You've been moving right along upstairs. It can't be long before paint and wallpaper," she said, hoping her voice didn't reflect her anxiety.

He slanted her a curious look as if realizing her thoughts had been elsewhere. Then he leaned back and said, "You're right…the part I like least. Especially wallpaper. I dread spending hours riffling through books trying to decide which patterns. And for six bedrooms, no less."

"I could help." *That's better.*

He looked at her with hope in his eyes. "How would you like to do the whole thing? I mean go to town and pick the paper. I'd hang it, of course."

"I'd love to. Actually, I'd enjoy hanging it, too." Nothing like hard work to defuse sexual tension. She attempted a guileless smile.

"Really? You've done this before?"

"Yes. It's fun…wallpapering, I mean." Of course wallpapering. What else would he think she meant?

"I'd pay you, of course."

She shook her head. "No. Absolutely not." She was glad she had finally found a way to make herself more useful.

"Don't be silly. I was prepared to pay a helper." When she started to protest again he cupped her chin and turned her face to meet his. "That was the job you came here for, right?" he said with a wink.

She chuckled and said, "Right, but—"

"What do I have to do to make you stop arguing with me?" He sounded teasing at first, but then she noticed he was staring at her lips, and any further attempt at conversation was lost.

It had been so long since that first kiss she'd wondered if another would ever happen, if he'd decided it had been a mistake. What she hadn't realized until today was how much she longed for him to do it again.

He moved closer, glancing up at her eyes…eyes she knew were betraying her need. And then his mouth was on hers. Tentatively at first. Until she leaned into him. Then he parted her lips on a groan and explored the wet recesses beyond.

Nicole felt the pulsing below her waist, a need she had denied for seven years. With a moan of her own she slid her tongue deeper in his mouth, feeling the distance closing between them. He broke the kiss long enough to pull her onto his lap, and then their mouths met again, more urgently. In her dizzy haze, she could feel his firmness pressing below her, and she squirmed against him. His breathing matched the hammering of her heart as he parted her thighs and slid a hand slowly upward. He kneaded her flesh as though his fingers fought their ultimate destination. She resisted the urge to push him higher, the wetness between her legs sure to tell him she wanted him as much as he wanted her.

By the time his thumb hooked the elastic of her panties and slid them lower she wanted to scream with desire. Never had a man been so patient, so tender. And it was driving her mad. Still, she held back, fighting the release that was sure to come. The pad of his thumb flicked mercilessly over her sensitive spot and she twitched beneath his touch. Finally his finger slid deep inside her and she heard a wild sound carry across the valley, one she didn't recognize as her own.

"Nicole, Nicole," he breathed into her neck. "Let it go, baby. Let it go."

A second finger joined the first and his hand moved faster. She cried out and trembled uncontrollably. And then she clung to him, waiting for air to fill her lungs. When she finally opened her eyes he was staring at her with a face so loving that she felt tears burn her eyes. He kissed her lips lightly this time and then he stood.

She wanted to ask where he was going, but it soon became apparent. He took the quilt that had been neatly folded against the back of the swing and snapped it open on the grass at the bottom of the steps. His movements were quick and sure now. And his gaze was intense, his breathing jagged as he picked her up and carried her from the porch.

Seven

Michael laid her gently on the blanket, kneeling at her side as he slowly unwrapped the gift she offered him. There were no surprises. He had studied her small waist and hips since she'd arrived, the generous curve of her breasts. Still, seeing her naked in the moonlight stole his breath away. He undressed quickly and stretched out alongside her, his head propped on a bent arm as he watched her quivering next to him.

"Someone really hurt you, baby, didn't he?" A tear trailed down her cheek, giving him the answer he already knew. "I'll never hurt you—"

She lifted her head and kissed him, a kiss so trusting and intimate he worried about lasting long enough to please her.

She pulled him to her as if she were afraid of thinking too much. Her body cried, Come to me before I change my mind. And he did, lowering himself atop her ever so gently, spreading her knees with his. With the length of him he rubbed her already-aroused, moist center, driving them both to the edge. Warm night air brushed over them as she splayed her fingers on his backside, nudging him closer, telling him now was the time.

Inch by inch he entered her, withdrawing slightly, penetrating farther until at last he was fully inside her. The beating of his heart matched the pulsing in his groin and he gritted his teeth. She held him close and kissed his neck, knowing not to move.

When he thought it was safe, the rhythm began. With each forward rock she arched into him, their bodies truly one. He slowed again, moving his mouth to her breast, kissing one extended nipple and then the other, her groans of pleasure driving him mad. He wanted the night to never end, to please her until she cried for mercy.

He trailed kisses down her stomach, his fingers now working her as she writhed beneath his touch. And when his mouth sucked her most sensitive spot she cried out his name. Her fingers dug into his shoulders and he wanted nothing more than to satisfy her. Hot liquid flowed over his hand and he groaned into her belly, her fingers raking his hair, then pulling him higher.

He straightened his arms and looked down at her, her eyes full of stars and love. They coupled again, this time faster, harder, her hot breath in his ear. With his hands beneath her bottom he drove into her one last time, spilling himself into her for a gloriously long time. Spent, he rolled to his side, taking her with him, never wanting to feel separate again.

As their bodies cooled, Michael pulled the quilt over them, Nicole tucked soundly under his arm. And in that instant he knew that at last he had found a woman he could trust, one he would love for the rest of his life.

Nicole awoke to the aroma of brewing coffee and rolled over on her back with a smile. She had usually been the one to awaken first and make breakfast, but this morning she hadn't even heard him stir. Sleep had been deep without the slightest reminder of the past or the reasons she had run from Denver. Last night's lovemaking had given her this gift.

Still feeling lethargic, she swung her legs over the side of the bed, noticing tender parts of her that had been neglected for so long. Perhaps what they had done had been a bit premature, yet she didn't feel any regret. The emotions were real for both of them; of that she was certain. And now, more than ever, hope surged through her veins that maybe this place…this man…could mark the beginning of a happy, full life.

She showered quickly and braided her wet hair, eager to see Michael. If she could persuade him to take a break from his work, she had decided what she would do. She would tell him about Cody. And then Robert.

In the kitchen she helped herself to a mug of coffee and practiced her words, butterflies turning in her stomach. He might be upset with her at first, but surely after he heard the whole story he would understand why she had hidden the truth, not just from him, but everyone.

Stalling a moment longer, she went to the refrigerator for orange juice and there, hanging from a magnet, was a message from Michael.

Nicole—
Went to the hardware store in Joeville. If I'm not back before you leave, have a great first day at your new job. I know you'll be terrific.

Michael

P.S. You look even more beautiful when you're sleeping.

Nicole pressed the note to her breast and felt her pulse start to race. She poured some juice and told herself to slow down, remembering how her impulsiveness in the past had led her down a long, dark road with Robert.

But Michael was different. Oh, so different. Still, it was just as well he wasn't here, she thought, grabbing a muffin and noticing the clock over the stove. She wanted to get to the ranch early and get acclimated. Besides, being apart the entire day would give her a chance to figure out how to tell Michael her story. They would have more time over a leisurely dinner. Already she pictured candles and serving something special.

Outside she walked briskly toward her old Chevy, pumped the pedal a half dozen times and then listened to it struggle to turn over. Earlier in the week she had made sure it would start and checked the gas level in case the day came that she would need it. There wasn't much gas left, but enough to get her to the ranch and back.

She headed out the gravel drive to the country road and then turned south for the ranch. The sun was burning off an early-morning fog, revealing layers of mountains to the west. Shades of blue-green turned to mauve, then green again, with patches of white snow looking like frosting that had been ladled on and allowed to randomly spill down the sides.

Nicole couldn't remember a time she had been happier. There wasn't a cloud in the sky, and she took this as a good sign that at last all would be well.

The twins were trailing behind Jenny to the east of the barn when Nicole pulled through the gate of the Malone ranch. As she made her way toward the main house she took in Jenny and Shane's cabin and a bunkhouse beyond that where hired hands were coming and going, either on horseback or in pickups. She parked between the barn and the main house just as Jenny reached the side door.

Jenny waved and smiled and took the girls by the hand. They seemed reticent about meeting their new sitter, but Nicole had expected this and greeted them warmly, without too much fuss, giving them time to get used to the idea.

"This is Sally," Jenny said, nudging one of the seven-year-olds out from behind Mom's legs. "And this is Sarah."

They said hi in unison, but kept their eyes cast down, running for the door as soon as they heard their cousins coming out.

The morning was a little strange for all of them, but by lunchtime things had relaxed. Nicole and her six charges sat around a large picnic table in the backyard while Hannah fussed with the lunch she had made and her famous chocolate chip cookies.

While the little ones finished eating, Hannah plopped down on the end of the bench next to Nicole and caught her breath.

"Whew. It's hotter 'n I thought out here." She fanned herself with an empty tray. "Sure could use some rain. Fields are mighty dry. Too dry, if ya ask me." And just as abruptly she set the tray down and turned toward Nicole. "How's things goin' over there at that Palace? You and Michael hittin' it off, are ya?"

Nicole blushed, thinking about last night, though this woman couldn't possibly know. Then she remembered Hannah talking with Molly at Taylor's party, and she knew this was probably standard procedure.

Hannah made a husky noise at the back of her throat and elbowed Nicole. "That good, huh? Guess you don't need my help then." With a hefty push off the table she pulled herself upright, her knees cracking in the process. "Well, ya jus' let me know if somebody needs a nudge." She winked before turning and waddling back indoors.

* * *

After lunch Nicole made a game out of rest time as many eager little hands helped make tents by stretching sheets over the clothesline in the backyard. Soft giggles and whispers reminded her of Cody, and she allowed a moment of sadness. Oh, how he would love the company of these children. Walter and Mabel were wonderful with him, but he was missing so much being there. And she was missing him.

Tomorrow, she told herself. She'd see him tomorrow. And tonight, after she told Michael... Did she dare to hope?

When the last of the children awoke and came out of the tent rubbing their eyes, they all trooped down to the stables to have a look at the new colt. Nicole rounded the corner and saw Max at the newborn's stall with his arm around Molly's shoulder. Nicole smiled. Obviously Hannah's magic was working.

On the drive back to the Palace, Nicole thought she was the luckiest girl in the world. Her first day of child care had ended without a hitch and she was going home to the dearest, most exciting man she had ever known. But as she pulled up the drive the tension started in her neck. Tonight she must tell Michael about her past and risk losing it all. No. She shook her head. He would understand.

Wouldn't he?

He was upstairs working when she walked in the front door, so she darted down the hall to freshen up before starting something special for dinner. But when she entered the kitchen Michael was on the phone.

"Sure, I'd love to. Just a sec." He put his hand over the receiver. "It's Josh. He has to fly into Billings for a few things. Want to ride along?"

"Not tonight. But you go ahead." She turned before he could see her disappointment. The sooner she got this over with, the better. Having hours alone to think about it wasn't going to make things easier.

"You sure?"

She walked to the refrigerator and started pulling out leftovers. "Positive."

Into the phone he said, "I'm ready whenever you are. Great. See you then." He hung up and came over to Nicole, hugging her around the waist from behind. It felt so cozy— just the two of them—here alone in the kitchen. It was all she could do not to beg him to stay. But another part of her worried about how he would react when he learned she'd deceived him.

"I could go another time. It's just that there are a few things I can't find locally—"

"It's okay. Really." She busied herself at the counter. If he was suspicious that something was wrong, he didn't show it.

There was barely time to finish their sandwiches and potato salad before Michael gave her a quick kiss and dashed out the door, promising to be home before dark.

When he returned, she had a bottle of wine chilling and thought she would suggest they take it out onto the porch. Then she would tell him everything.

But he no sooner carried his supplies inside than there was a timid knock at the front door. Curious, Nicole followed Michael to see who it was.

And there stood Walter, Cody cradled in his frail, shaking arms.

Nicole pushed by Michael and opened the screen, taking Cody from him. When she saw no blood, no broken bones she exhaled, feeling foolish for thinking such dreadful thoughts. If he'd been hurt, Walter would have taken him to the hospital, not here.

"I'm sorry ta barge in like this, Nicole..."

Michael opened the door, inviting the old man inside. He

looked at the two strangers and then Nicole, waiting for some explanation.

"It's all right, Walter." She looked sheepishly at Michael before making introductions. "This is Michael Phillips—the man I work for. Michael, this is Walter Williams. He and his wife, Mabel, have been caring for—" she swallowed hard; this wasn't how she'd wanted him to hear "—caring for Cody...my son."

In the space of a heartbeat Nicole watched Michael's expression change from shock to pain to anger. His jaw muscles were working hard as he struggled for control. Giving Nicole one last seething glare, he turned to Walter.

"Please come in." He extended his arm to the sofa where Nicole was laying Cody, but Walter just stood in the doorway, twisting the rim of his hat in his gnarled fingers.

"Thanks, but I'd better be going. My wife is in the hospital."

Nicole rushed to him, forgetting her own problems for the moment. "Oh, Walter. What's wrong?"

"She fell and broke her hip." He peered around her to Cody, still sleeping soundly. "Our little man called 911 and then came and found me in the woods. You woulda been proud of him, missy."

"Which hospital is she at?" Nicole asked, unable to meet Michael's eyes.

"Bozeman. Suspect she'll be there a while. But they say she'll be okay in time."

Walter started to walk outside and Nicole followed him. Over his shoulder he said, "Nice meetin' ya, Mr. Phillips. Nicole been sayin' lots of good things about you and this place."

Nicole didn't look at Michael's face, certain what she would see.

With one hand on the door handle to his truck, Walter stopped and turned. "Oh, there's somethin' else ya need to know. This mornin', at the doughnut shop, I overheard talk of a stranger in a big Cadillac lookin' for a woman and a boy.''

Nicole felt the blood drain from her head, the ground uneven beneath her feet. No! Not after all this time. It couldn't be. Yet it had to—

She retraced her time up north. She'd been careful not to take Cody with her anywhere. Even if she fit the description and someone said so, they couldn't say there was a child with her. She'd even been homeschooling him because of this very fear.

"I'm sorry ta be the bearer of bad news," Walter said, as he opened the door. "I tried callin', but well…I hope showin' up like this ain't gonna be a big problem—''

"Hush now, old friend. You did the right thing. Don't you worry about Michael. He'll get used to the idea eventually. I was going to tell him tonight, anyway.''

"Really? You're not just sayin' that ta make me feel better, now are ya?''

"Really.'' She gave him a hard hug. "Give Mabel my love. Tell her I'll be saying some prayers for her, that I'll get up to see her as soon as I can. Does she have a phone?''

"Yes, she does. Right on the bed railing so she don't have ta move or nothing. Her roommate even got a TV, so Mabel can watch her soaps and everything.''

"Tell her I'll call her tomorrow. What about you? Are you okay?''

He stepped behind the wheel of his rusty old pickup. "I miss her somethin' awful, but otherwise I'm fine.''

"Oh, wait. I'll be right back.'' She ran inside and back, handing him a few folded dollars.

"No, missy. You keep it.'' He started to hand it back, but she tightened his fingers around it.

"I insist. I wish it could be more, but this will help with gas…getting to and from the hospital.''

In the end Walter accepted and they said their goodbyes. Nicole watched as the pickup chugged down the drive, and she dreaded going back inside, knowing what mood she'd find Michael in. She sucked in a deep breath and decided she'd start by putting Cody in her bed. At least she could spare her son the argument that was sure to come.

"Michael…let me explain."

"There's nothing to explain. I trusted another woman. My fault."

"Michael, please. Talk to me."

"I have nothing to say to you, Nicole." He pushed out the screen door, letting it slam between them.

Sure he had cause to be angry, but his stubbornness was pushing her limits. She followed him as far as the porch and then yelled after him. "Go ahead. Run away. Just like you did seven years ago." The words were no sooner out of her mouth than she regretted them. She was sure they were true, but this wasn't how she meant for it to come out.

He bounded back to her, stopping inches from her face. "Look who's calling the kettle black. What are *you* running from, Miss Perfect. You got a husband out there somewhere, too?"

Unshed tears threatened to choke her as she shook her head from side to side.

"And about what happened here seven years ago…you haven't a clue—"

"I know it had something to do with Max," she returned, deciding she would finish what she had started. He flinched and backed up a step, not denying her words. "And I know everyone loves Max, so whatever it is, I wish you'd deal with it—"

"You got a lot of nerve." He gripped her arms and pulled her closer, his hot breath and angry glare reminding her of another man years ago, and she felt herself tremble. "I trusted you, Ms. Bedder—or whatever your name is— or last night wouldn't have happened." He was staring at her lips, his breathing labored, an inner struggle tightening his jaw.

Nicole swallowed hard. "I was going to tell you—"

"Don't make it worse."

"Listen to me. Please. You were gone when I got up this morning and then Josh called after I got back. There just wasn't time."

"Why didn't you tell me last night?"

"I didn't want to ruin things. Everything was so perfect." She saw a shadow of doubt pass over his eyes, and then he let go of her and crossed his arms.

"How do I know you're not just saying this...now that you got caught?"

"You don't know." She touched his arm lightly, surprised when he didn't shrug her off. "Michael...you just have to trust me."

It was as if she'd slapped him awake. "Trust?" He pushed her hand away and sneered at her, his upper lip curling in an unflattering way. Then he turned and stalked toward his van. "You're just like—" He flung open the door and didn't finish.

"Like who?" she called out too softly, feeling defeated. He didn't answer. She didn't expect him to.

She wanted to go after him, but she didn't. Something told her to give him space, to let him cool off. Maybe later—when she explained about Cody—maybe then Michael would understand and share the missing pieces of his own life, too.

Somehow she would convince him that she wasn't like the others—at least not like whoever had caused him such pain.

She went back inside and sat in front of the bay window

in the parlor, calming herself and trying to put things into perspective. Cody's arrival had shocked him, justifiably so. It didn't help that this had happened the day after they had made love.

Nicole turned and crossed her arms over the back of the love seat. Resting a cheek against her arms she stared at the stars and thought about last night. As magical as it had been, had it happened too soon? Just a little more time and she would have told him everything, and then things would be different now. It wouldn't have changed his shock when he learned about Cody, but it may not have felt like such a personal betrayal.

She rehashed their harsh words and then released a long sigh. It didn't take a rocket scientist to know trust was a big issue with Michael. Now it would take a lot to win it back. But she had time, didn't she? It would be a while before the house was done and she would win his trust in that time if it was the last thing she did.

But what if he asked her to leave? She mulled on this one only a moment. No. He knew Taylor and the others needed her. And besides, if he had taken her in that first day when she needed help, he certainly wouldn't put her out now with a child.

But suddenly the prospect of staying seemed almost as frightening. Perhaps tonight's scene had been the reality check she needed. What had she been thinking... encouraging Michael the way she had?

She buried her face in her arms, the image of them on the quilt too vivid in her mind. Never had it felt so right.

But it wasn't.

Unless she was prepared to make a commitment to stay, she had no business letting Michael think differently. The sad truth was as long as Robert was out there on the loose, she and Cody had to be ready to run at any moment...which would mean leaving Michael. His life savings was tied up in this house, and even if it was already finished and sold he would want to live near Taylor and her family. She couldn't ask him to go with her. And there was no way she could commit to stay. Not forever, anyway.

Feeling the weight of the world, she shuffled down the hall and checked on Cody. Then she covered herself with an afghan on the sofa in the next room, hoping sleep would temporarily ease the pain in her heart.

But sleep eluded her, and she lay staring into the night, thinking. It was important that Michael learn to trust her again, that he know how much he meant to her, that last night wasn't some meaningless dalliance. Of all this she was certain. But beyond that, she didn't know. It would take a miracle for the happy-ever-after of her dreams.

And so, hours later, when she still couldn't sleep, a miracle was what she prayed for.

Eight

After an hour of driving nowhere, Michael found himself in Taylor's driveway, trying to rein in his temper as his sister spotted him and ran to his open window.

"Michael! What's wrong?"

He opened the door and stepped out, resisting the urge to slam it behind him, mindful of the sleeping children in the house. In his mind's eye he saw another sleeping child, an innocent in the midst of all this turmoil back at the Palace.

"Come sit with me on the porch," she said, taking his hand.

"Where's Josh?"

"Sound asleep." She sat on the top step and pulled him down next to her. "When was the last time we had a long talk? Just the two of us?"

"Not since you came home for Dad's funeral a couple of years ago." He could feel the fight going out of him at the mention of his father's name. "I miss him, Taylor. A lot."

She squeezed his hand. "I do, too." She let go of him and turned sideways, leaning her back against a post. "But that's not what's on your mind, is it?"

It was a statement, not a question. She knew him well. "No. It's not."

"Am I going to have to play Twenty Questions?"

He hunched forward and folded his hands between his knees. Where did he start? Certainly not with his feelings for Nicole. He wasn't ready for that. Then maybe the arrival of Nicole's son, who he didn't know existed until an hour ago. Or maybe Max. Hell, he just didn't know.

He ran his hand through his hair and shook his head in confusion. Driving the back roads at reckless speeds had done nothing but resurrect unresolved issues, issues he had hoped would go away if ignored.

Taylor spoke in a gentle voice. "Michael...you know, all these years we've never talked about Max, how you feel. It must be harder now that you're living so close."

He nodded slowly, grateful that his sister had taken the lead. "What's hard is that he seems to be an okay guy. I wish I could hate him. It would be a lot easier."

"Would it?"

He shrugged, not knowing what to think. His mind was mush. "Maybe if I had known when I was younger...if Mom had told me before she died."

"We can't blame Max for that. He learned the truth the same time as we did."

"I know. Which leaves me only Mom to be angry with. And I don't like that, either. Not a bit." Taylor came closer and rested her head on his shoulder. He could sense she was weighing her next words carefully.

"You know, it's hard for us to think of our parents as

regular human beings—people with dreams and hopes and...and even desires.''

He nodded slowly and uncrossed his arms, not at all comfortable talking about his mother's intimate life.

"They were so different. Mom loved her movies and books. Nothing against Dad, little brother, but when did he ever go to a movie or read a book?''

"And that's supposed to justify having an affair?'' he snapped, knowing it wasn't his sister's fault yet needing to vent.

"No. But, Michael, she paid for that mistake the rest of her life. And she did what she thought was right by staying with Dad and keeping the family together.'' She patted his knee and sighed. "Listen, I'm not trying to sell you on anything. It's just that if you had read what I read I think you might have forgiven her and Max. Oh, Michael. If only I hadn't burned those journals.''

Michael slid his arm around his sister's waist and pulled her closer. "I would have done the same thing, sis.'' He kissed her forehead and they held each other for a while and rocked. When she finally pulled away and leaned back against the post, he remembered what had really driven him from the house tonight. And it had nothing to do with Max. At least not initially.

"Nicole was wonderful with the children today,'' Taylor said after a moment.

Michael turned toward Taylor and leaned against the opposite post. His sister was smiling a Cheshire cat smile, as if she knew Nicole was on his mind. How did she do that, he wondered? Was he that transparent?

"I'm so glad you introduced us, little brother. She's a real godsend.''

He crossed his arms as well as his ankles and looked away. "Yeah, right.''

"Michael?'' She chuckled softly, and out of the corner

of his eye he could see her shaking her head and smiling. "Are you smitten with Nicole?"

"There's nothing funny about this, Taylor." Suddenly restless, he stood and walked down the steps. He hadn't meant to sound so curt, but damn it—

"Okay," she said, a little bite to her tone. "Then why don't you tell me about it. That's what you *really* came here for, isn't it?"

With hands on hips he let the tension seep out of his lungs. "Damn, I hate it when you're right." He looked over his shoulder, and Taylor was smiling at him, not a smile of victory, but one so serene that he envied her her inner calm.

Resigned, he sat back down and told her everything—everything except the fact that he had made love to Nicole. Some things he held close. This was one of them. Yet he did tell her how he had come to care about Nicole and to even trust her. Finally he told of her son arriving tonight and the betrayal that had stirred in his gut.

When he'd finished, Taylor asked, "How did she explain things?"

"She didn't. Well…she tried, but I didn't want to hear more lies."

"When did she ever lie to you?"

"Okay. Sins of omission. In my book I don't see a lot of difference. She misled me and that's enough. Besides, what kind of mother would leave her child and go looking for work at what she thought was the Purple Palace?"

"Probably a very desperate one." Taylor leaned in closer, resting a hand on her brother's arm. "Michael, you see how she is with children. It can't be that she doesn't love her own son. Why don't you hear her out?"

He stepped off the porch again and paced as he shook his head. "What's the point? I can't trust her."

"Michael, every woman is not Roxanne. I know it hurt

you when you learned she'd been cheating on you, but thank God you found out before you married her. Besides—"

He started walking back toward the van. She got up and followed.

"Where are you going?"

"I thought you'd understand."

Taylor raced to his side and gripped his arm, but he refused to turn around. "I *do* understand."

He got into the van and looked down at her. "First Mom lies, then Roxanne cheats, now Nicole deceives. I know you mean well, sis. But besides you, I don't know of a woman alive I would trust." He threw the gearshift into reverse and sped down the drive, spewing gravel and dust in his wake.

From his side window he saw his sister standing in the shadow of the porch light, and he cursed aloud.

The one woman who had never failed him and he'd acted like a jerk.

The next morning Michael showered and dressed quickly, hoping to grab some coffee and head upstairs before Nicole could leave her room. But as soon as he opened his door he heard the sound of the young boy's voice coming from the kitchen.

He swore under his breath. This was his house, yet he felt no control. No options had come to him during the long night that would free him of this problem. None that his conscience could live with, anyway. His sister, and now Jenny and Savannah, were excited about Nicole's help. He wouldn't be the one to burst their bubble. He strode down the hall, righteously hanging on to his anger like a shield. He'd just have to suck it in until the house was finished and sold. Then Nicole would be someone else's problem.

He crossed to the cupboard, got a mug and filled it without looking at the source of his frustration.

"Good morning," Nicole said, her eyes cast down.

"Hi, Mr. Phillips. You got a really neat house."

Michael exhaled loudly as he turned, reminding himself this boy had done nothing to earn his foul mood. He had his mother's eyes, Michael noticed. And her infectious smile. "You like it, huh?"

He nodded enthusiastically. "And what a cool bed!"

Michael found a bagel and dropped it into the toaster. If the boy had slept in the bed, he wondered where Nicole had slept. He took cream cheese from the refrigerator as he tried to block the image of her in *any* bed from his mind. The bagel popped up and he wanted to throw it across the room.

"Michael?"

He spread cream cheese and didn't look up. "Hmm?"

"I stocked up on enough groceries last Wednesday that I don't think we need anything today. Just milk and a couple of things I can get in Joeville."

He pulled his money clip from his jeans pocket and slapped it on the counter. "Take what you need."

"Well…actually, I was thinking of skipping it today and helping you."

He stilled his hands and brought his head up, meeting her eyes for the first time.

Nicole looked away first, resting her hand on the boy's head. "Cody, why don't you go outside and play. I'll be out in a few minutes."

Michael watched the boy look from one adult to the other as he slid off his chair and headed for the door. Wouldn't you know the kid would be well behaved. "Cody?"

He stopped and turned, one hand on the doorknob. "Yes, sir?"

"There's a horse in the barn…if you want to go see

her.'' The familiar brown eyes grew rounder. "Her name is Mae.''

The sound of sneakers running across the porch and down the path brought an involuntary smile to Michael's face.

"Thank you, Michael.''

His smile disappeared and he took a bite of bagel. He had a mind to turn on his heel and head upstairs, but there was no time better than the present to establish some ground rules, so he set his bagel aside and leaned back against the counter.

"Look, Nicole, I got a house to finish, you got kids to take care of. If we stay out of each other's way it's possible we could get through this and still be civil.''

She nodded. "I agree.''

Where was the elaborate story she had pleaded with him to hear last night? She was just sitting there, cool as a cucumber. Then she finished her coffee and stood.

"I was thinking that today would be the perfect time to start the wallpaper project. I could take Cody with me and look through books. With so many rooms, that could be an all-day job. What do you think?''

What did he think? He thought he must be losing his mind. The anger he'd vowed to hang on to was already slipping. "But it's Wednesday. Today's your day off.''

She shrugged. "It's just another day...now that Cody's with me.''

Now that he knew how she had spent her time away, he wondered if she'd ever bothered to apply for work elsewhere. Was it her plan all along to stay here? If so, was seducing him part of that plan, too? He recalled how things had unfolded on the swing two nights ago. He had been the one to put his arm around her and pull her close. He had been the one to lower his mouth—

This line of thinking wasn't smart.

"Michael?"

"Sure. Why not? Keep track of your time." He grabbed his bagel and coffee and headed for the stairs. Nicole was right behind him. Now what did she want?

"I'll just get some measurements and be on my way."

"I have a set of blueprints you could use instead." He took the stairs two at a time and found the prints, anxious for her to be gone. He handed her the long roll. "Here you go. Have at it. Oh, and take the van. I won't be needing it." She didn't take the blueprints immediately, forcing him to look at her.

"Would you like me to bring back samples for you to choose from?"

Her eyes seemed sad, almost begging for forgiveness. He had to look away.

"No. You choose. I tr—" The word *trust* caught in his throat. He *did* trust her to decorate, yet he couldn't bring himself to use that word, not this morning. "Whatever you decide, I'm sure will be fine." He buckled on his tool belt and listened to her thin acknowledgment as she retreated softly down the stairs.

A few minutes later Michael heard little feet running across the porch and then the crunch of gravel as the van drove away. Weary from lack of sleep, he sat on the floor, leaned against the wall and closed his eyes.

Nicole, Nicole. How was he supposed to get her out of his system when the sight and scent of her surrounded him daily? She probably did have a good explanation for deceiving him, but damn it, why hadn't she trusted him enough to tell him the truth? If not at first, then after their night together. Again the images swirled and consumed him—the feel of her in his arms, his lips on hers, their bodies as one.

He sprang from the floor and picked up a hammer. Work was his only salvation. And the sooner he finished this place, the sooner they would go their separate ways and he could forget her.

"Right," he muttered between clenched teeth, and drove in a nail with three resounding strikes.

Nine

Two weeks later Nicole asked Michael if he would linger over breakfast and discuss projects around the house. As difficult as it had been to work with her in such close proximity, he had to admit she was contributing in more ways than he had expected. She'd painted most of the trim upstairs, which was tedious work that he couldn't have done as well or with as much patience. And all of her suggestions had been valuable, too, each one improving the end result.

If only she didn't have to look so good. Or act so sweet. Or be such a good mother. Or all the other things that made her so damnably appealing. At times it was difficult to remember why he was angry with her. It was as though she were doing her best to prove she could be trusted. She hadn't tried *explaining* anything, yet she seemed hell-bent on demonstrating her point. Which, when he was honest with himself, he had to admit she was doing quite nicely.

Nicole refilled both their cups, gave Cody a second cinnamon roll and then sat down across the table. "I've been thinking about the papering. I wonder if we should put it off a little longer," she said.

"Why's that?" He eyed her over the rim of his mug, trying not to notice the healthy glow of her skin or the streaks of sun that highlighted her fair hair.

"I thought I could rip out carpet first. It's bound to stir up a lot of dust."

"You're probably right, but that's a pretty heavy job." He rocked back in his chair and thought before he spoke. "It's a two-person job...at least carrying the rolls down the stairs is."

"I could help," Cody said, sitting taller in his chair.

Nicole smiled at her son. "I bet you could, big guy, but I think it will take more muscle than the two of us." She hesitated, then looked at Michael. "Now that school's out I was wondering if Billy might help. He offered last time I was at the ranch."

Michael nodded. "Not a bad idea." Then why was he feeling let down that she wasn't hinting *he* be the one to help her? Still, working apart was what he wanted, wasn't it? It didn't seem quite as clear these days. Without realizing when or how, they had become a team, complementing each other at every turn. And now he couldn't help but wonder if there could be more.

"Maybe the hardwood floors down here should be sanded first, too."

The floors. Yes. Concentrate on the floors. This had been another thing they had discussed and agreed upon. The upstairs guest rooms should be recarpeted for a more quiet and cozy feel, but the first-floor foyer, parlor and dining room floors would be refinished, and the oriental rugs left behind by the previous owners would be cleaned and put to good use in those areas.

"For sure," Michael said. "Another thing Billy could

help with.'' Feeling a sudden need to expend some energy, he pushed out his chair and paced to the phone hanging on the wall. ''Think I'll give him a call now. See if I can catch him.''

''Actually, he's coming over later today.''

Michael hung up the receiver and eyed her levelly. Had she already asked him? Without checking with him first?

As if reading his mind, she said, ''I didn't say a word about this. I thought you should be the one to ask.''

He picked up his mug and drank more coffee, hoping she didn't notice the guilt on his face. How quickly he jumped to the wrong conclusion whenever a woman surprised him. Probably because it usually wasn't good news. Yet ever since Cody's arrival Michael hadn't seen a single reason to doubt Nicole's motives. Was it all an act? He remembered the day she'd come about the job and the act she'd put on then. He suppressed a smile. No, she wasn't that good an actress.

Out of the corner of his eye, Michael noticed Cody stealing peeks at him. Finally the boy spoke in a shy, quiet voice. ''Billy's going to take me riding today...if it's okay with you, Mr. Phillips.''

What kind of ogre had he been these past weeks for the boy to look so frightened? True, he hadn't allowed a bond to develop, not when he knew it would be broken all too soon. It could only hurt the boy. But there was no reason for him to be afraid. ''Of course it's okay, Cody. Billy can come over anytime he wants.''

With his gaze lowered, Cody said, ''Thank you,'' before tugging on his mother's sleeve and asking, ''May I be excused?''

Nicole handed him a napkin and he wiped traces of juice from his upper lip. ''Yes, you may.''

''Can I help tear up carpet with you, Mama?'' She

smiled and nodded approval, and then he raced off as if chased by a pack of wolves.

Nicole cleared the table while Michael made a call to the hardware store. When he hung up he started for the stairs. He needed space to sort things out. This polite routine of theirs wasn't working for him anymore. They needed to talk. Soon. But first he had to think.

Before he reached the first step he heard the whispered words of Cody down the hall, and then he backtracked. The boy had seemed extra edgy this morning, and Michael couldn't help but think he had something to do with it, so he decided to wait and listen.

"He's not the man in the picture, is he, Mama?"

"Who, Cody?"

"Mr. Phillips."

"Cody! Of course not. Why would you think that?"

"Sometimes he scares me. Well, not really scares me. But he looks mad at me or something."

"Come here, big guy."

Around the corner Michael held his breath. He listened to Nicole's gentle words of assurance, and he was tempted to reveal himself and convince Cody he had done nothing wrong. In fact, he was a great kid. But he stood riveted in place, uncertainty and guilt swallowing his tongue.

"He's not mad at you, Cody," Nicole said. "I'm the one who made him angry."

"Why? What did you do?"

"I...well, I wasn't completely honest with him before you came, but everything's okay now, sweetie. You have nothing to worry about."

Michael started to move, feeling uncomfortable eavesdropping and thinking he had heard enough, but something made him wait a little longer.

"That man in the picture doesn't know where we are. We're safe here, sweetheart. Believe me."

"Okay," Cody said, not sounding sure. "But why doesn't Mr. Phillips like me?"

"Oh, Cody. I'm sure he likes you. He's just so busy working, that's all. Now come on. Give me a big hug and let me see a smile."

Michael raced quietly up the stairs, shut the door to the first bedroom behind him and listened to the hammering of his heart in his ears.

That man in the picture doesn't know where we are. We're safe here.

The thought of anyone hurting Nicole and Cody left acid from this morning's coffee burning in his chest. What man? What had the guy done to make them so afraid? And now that he knew, how could he protect them?

He started pacing the length of the room, filled with rage at a faceless man who could have caused any woman or child pain...especially *this* woman and child!

He stopped at the window and raked his fingers through his hair. There was no point denying his feelings any longer. His anger might have blinded him for a while. Then he might have convinced himself he could work side by side with Nicole and nothing more. But now he had to admit he'd deluded himself. He wanted more. Much more.

He paced again. Whatever wrong Nicole had done, it didn't hold a candle to his own stubborn pride. What was important now was to protect her and Cody. But how? And from whom? One way or the other he would find out.

It was midafternoon when Michael heard Cody running down the stairs and out the front door. Michael watched and listened from an upstairs bedroom overlooking the porch as Billy tied his paint pony to a hitching post and asked Cody for something to drink. Cody said his mom had just made lemonade and Billy suggested they have some and sit for a while before their ride.

Michael noticed Billy didn't go inside. He sat down on the step and looked around, his gaze catching and holding here and there. Working here might be tougher than Michael had considered. The young man's memories of this place had to be painful.

Cody came out with two glasses held carefully in front of him, handed one to Billy and sat down beside him. They drank and didn't speak for a while. Michael finished caulking a new window he'd been working on and moved to a second on the same side of the house.

Billy set his glass down and leaned forward on his thighs. "You know...I used to live here when I was your age."

"Mom told me. Your bed is way-y-y cool."

Billy looked back at the boy. "I hope you're happy here, Cody. I was."

"Most of the time—" Cody started, then stopped. Michael looked down from above as the boy twisted his ankles nervously from side to side.

"If something's wrong, you can tell me, Cody."

"Well...it's just that—" He bent over and grabbed the toes of both shoes and kept his head down. "I think Mr. Phillips wishes I wasn't around."

For the second time today Michael felt a kick in his gut. Cody wasn't to blame for any of the tension in this house. Fortunately that is exactly what Billy told him.

"When I first went to live with Dad and Savannah I felt the same way. I even ran away once."

"Really? Weren't you scared?"

"Shaking in my boots. But I was so wrong, Cody. Dad and Savannah had some things to work out between them that had absolutely nothing to do with me."

Michael put down his caulk gun and walked away from the window. He'd heard enough. If his conscience pricked any deeper it would bleed. How could he not have seen the effect his behavior was having on Cody? He was just a kid.

An innocent kid. How could a kid understand the screwed-up world of the adults around him?

Well, enough was enough. It was time to undo some of the wrongs. He unbuckled his tool belt, set it on the floor and went downstairs, hoping his idea was a good one.

The pair had just finished their drinks and were rinsing their glasses in the kitchen sink when Michael joined them.

"Billy." Michael crossed the room with his hand extended. "I was going to call you today. Glad you're here."

Billy shook Michael's hand and stepped back. "Need a hand?"

"As a matter of fact, I do. But not now. I could use a break and was hoping to tag along with you guys. I don't get much time with old Mae." Michael caught the look of astonishment on Cody's face and wasn't surprised. It had been all work and no play around here. That was about to change.

"Sounds great. Except…well, we'll be one horse short."

"No problem. Cody can ride with me." Michael saw the disappointed look on Cody's face. Surely he had been looking forward to riding a horse of his own. The solution came easily. They could ride over to Max's and get a third horse. Regardless of his feelings for Max, it was time to put Cody's needs first—something he should have thought of long before this.

"Cody?" Michael said, looking directly at the boy. "You don't mind riding with me, do you?"

The boy stared at his shoes, his bottom lip starting to quiver. "No, Mr. Phillips."

Michael stooped to Cody's level. "I'd rather you call me Michael…if that's okay with you." Cody looked up, his eyes still sad. "And if Billy thinks it's okay, I thought maybe we could ride over to the ranch and borrow a horse for you to ride all by yourself awhile."

Cody spun toward Billy, the freckles spattered across the

bridge of his nose and cheeks exaggerated by his flushed face. "Can we, Billy?"

Billy studied Michael, seeming as surprised as Cody by the suggestion, but for different reasons. "It's a great idea."

"Let me check with Nicole and I'll be right back."

Billy rested a hand on Cody's shoulder and headed for the barn. "Come on. Let's go get Mae saddled up."

Nicole watched the trio ride off, surprised that Cody was riding with Michael and not Billy. Why was Michael making this sudden effort with Cody, especially now that their work was drawing to an end? At first she had wished that the two would become close, but now it would only make leaving here harder.

The thought of leaving caused a heavy weight to press against her chest. This had been a safe place to hide, and with each day's work she had fallen more and more in love with this old house.

But it was more than the house; she couldn't pretend otherwise. It was the man who owned it. Walking away from Michael and the life she fantasized about each night as she listened to him moving about in the next room seemed impossible now. And the longer she stayed, the more it would hurt.

Perhaps it would be best for all of them if she and Cody moved on. Soon. But how would she ever find the courage to say goodbye?

She closed her eyes and said a silent prayer. *Please, Lord. Help me do the right thing. But if there's any way we can stay...*

Cody wiggled in the saddle trying to find a comfortable spot, his legs spread so wide across Mae's girth that he appeared almost to be doing the splits.

If this bothered Cody, it was not obvious as the horses

plodded along a path leading toward the ranch, the boy stroking Mae's mane often and, for the most part, leaning forward in what seemed to Michael an attempt to avoid contact with him. He couldn't blame the little guy. Before today he hadn't made any effort to get close. Michael tried not to dwell on this as they rode along, but the uncomfortable thought was never far from his mind.

Michael told Billy about work on the house, including the carpet removal and floor sanding, and as was the case with most teens Michael knew, Billy jumped at the chance for some extra spending money. He said he could begin tomorrow.

"What about painting? I could help with that, too."

"Nicole's been working on that. And as soon as the sanding is done, she's ready to start wallpapering."

"I was thinking more about the outside. I don't know how Nicole feels about heights, but there's some pretty high peaks."

"My mom hates ladders. She had to get one of my balsa wood airplanes off the roof once and her legs were *really* shaking."

Michael heard the concern in the boy's voice and wanted to squeeze him for it. His love for his mother was unabashed...as was hers for him. Another pang of guilt shot through him. Evidence of Nicole's true character was right under his nose all along, yet his stubborn pride or male ego or...or whatever it was...had kept him at arm's length all these weeks. For what? To protect himself or to punish her? Either way, it was time things changed. After what he'd overheard this morning, there should be no doubt she had her reasons for secrecy. Besides, he missed her.

The horses stopped to nibble on a patch of tall grass and to drink from the narrow stream that trickled from the ranch down the hillside, emptying into a small lake a couple miles south of the Palace. Michael looked over at Billy, who was taking in his surroundings and seeming very content.

"Do you ever get used to this?" Michael asked, his arm making a sweeping motion at the vast beauty that treated the eye in all directions.

Billy shook his head, gazing out at the mountains on the horizon and the miles of unspoiled land. "I don't think I'll ever leave Montana. Can't imagine being packed in like sardines in some polluted city. Lots of clean air and space—that's more to my liking." The horses finished and they ambled on. "I like not having to lock our doors, too. It feels safe here, know what I mean?"

It was a rhetorical question, so Michael was surprised when Cody said, "I do." Then he added, "But I hope the bad man stays far away."

Billy asked what Michael was thinking. "What bad man, Cody?"

The boy squirmed in the saddle and didn't answer right away. The only sound for minutes was the clopping of the horses' hooves against the hard-packed, dry earth.

Michael was about to repeat the question when Cody said, "Mama told Grandpa Walter and Grandma Mabel. They're our special friends."

It was obvious he wanted to talk about it, but Michael sensed the boy's reluctance. "We're friends, too, Cody. It's safe to tell us."

Cody turned his head and eyed Michael, then looked over at Billy as if taking both men's measure. Trust apparently came slowly with Cody, too, and snippets of what Michael had heard this morning came back. He didn't want to admit to the boy that he'd been eavesdropping, yet suddenly it seemed all-important that he know more about the man in the picture.

"Cody, I know I wasn't supposed to hear this, but you

seemed worried about some man in a picture you were showing your mom this morning. Is that the bad man?''

Cody nodded slowly, his little body inching back toward the protection of Michael, who longed to wrap his arm around the boy and pull him close. Yet he didn't want to rush things, so he didn't, encouraging the words to flow instead. ''Can you tell us about him, Cody?''

''He just got out of jail...and Mama says he's looking for us. That's why we were hiding at Grandma and Grandpa's. They're not really my grandma and grandpa, but Mama said I could call them that. They let us stay with them when we didn't have any money. But they were really old, and Mama said she had to find a job. That's when she came here.''

Billy pressed further. ''What did this bad man do?''

''He robbed a store with a big gun, but a policeman caught him and put him in jail.''

''Did you or your mom see the robbery?'' Billy asked, jumping to the same conclusion as Michael. If either of them witnessed the act and testified against this guy, maybe he was after revenge.

Cody shook his head. ''No. I wasn't even borned. But Mama heard about it.''

''Then why would he be looking for you and your mom? Do you know?''

Cody looked away, his voice barely audible. ''Because...because he's my dad.''

Michael closed his eyes, pain shooting right to his heart. Unable to restrain himself any longer, he tugged Cody back in the saddle and held him tight. He came without resistance, leaning into him with all his weight.

''Mama said if I ever see him I should run and hide.''

''Good advice, guy.'' No wonder Nicole had been so secretive. The sweet scent of Cody's hair drifted up, and

Michael shuddered at the possibility of any harm coming
to this innocent child.

Or Nicole.

Who was back at the house.

Alone.

Fear gripped the pit of his stomach. Should they turn
around and head back now? Was this creep anywhere
around? He looked straight ahead and could see the ranch.
It was closer than turning back. As soon as he got there he
would use the phone and call Nicole. He could borrow a
truck and get back faster than on Mae. He glanced over at
Billy, whose pinched expression said he was having similar
thoughts.

"What say we give these old horses a little workout?"
Billy asked, and dug in his heels. Michael nudged Mae into
a slow trot, and before long they were at the barn.

Hannah was resting on an old glider in the backyard, a
Bible open in her lap. She seemed shocked to see Michael
approaching, but at first sight of Cody, her plump arms
extended wide and he went to her.

Billy said he'd tend to the horses if Michael wanted to
use the phone. Not needing any coaxing, Michael opened
the screen door leading to the kitchen and went inside.
Thankful that no one was around, he crossed straight for
the phone on the wall and punched in the number. He
counted. Four, five, six. He growled in frustration, hung up
and dialed more carefully, hoping he'd made an error the
first time.

Again it rang and rang.

Ten

On the ninth ring, short of breath, Nicole ran in from the garden and caught the phone, instantly detecting the fear in Michael's voice.

"Is something wrong with Cody?" Her pulse raced faster; it was hard to swallow.

"No, Cody's fine. He's visiting with Hannah."

Nicole exhaled loudly, pulled up a chair and sat down. She looked at her hands. They were filthy from tearing up carpet and weeding the garden. But more than that they were shaking. A day of physical exertion had done nothing to ease the prospect of leaving Michael. And now she had imagined the reappearance of Robert, forcing her hand. She had to stop this.

But when Michael told her where to find his shotgun and ammunition, she sat up with a jolt.

"Why are you telling me this?"

"Cody told me about—" there was a long pause, and then "—about the man in the picture he's afraid of."

Surprisingly she felt a measure of relief.

"Would you like us to come back right away? We could borrow a truck—"

"Thank you, Michael, but no. The only ones who know I'm here are Walter and Mabel and they'd never tell. I'm okay." She could hear Michael sighing at the other end of the phone and she was touched by this unexpected show of concern. If only she could convince herself that she and Cody were safe, that they would never be found here. Sadly, she knew she couldn't.

But this wasn't a conversation she wanted to have on the phone, so she changed the subject. "How did Cody do on Mae? I bet he's having a great time."

"He is." There was silence, then he added, "He's a great kid, Nicole. I should have told you that a long time ago. You've done a wonderful job with him."

Stunned, she didn't know quite what to say except another feeble thank-you. More than anything he might have said, this was the highest compliment. Yet it did nothing but make her feel sad. Michael would have made such a wonderful father....

Would have. Past tense. It was as if her decision had already been made, that she had given up all hope. While her heart was screaming *No!* logic took a foothold.

When she fell silent Michael said, "If you're certain you're okay, then we'll be home in about two hours. Don't fuss with dinner, okay?" There was a pause and then he added, "Later...can we talk?"

He didn't have to say about what. All she could manage was a weak "Yes" before she hung up the phone and stared sightlessly out the window.

It was her past he would want to know about...that he deserved to know...that she had wanted to tell him about as soon as she'd realized how much she cared.

Robert. The mere thought of him made her cringe. She

wondered for a moment if she should have mentioned what Walter had said—that Robert had been seen at the dough-nut shop asking questions—but that would have only worried him more. Besides, nothing had come of it, anyway.

Yet. She couldn't shake the fear that he was close and getting closer. Was this her way of pushing herself into a decision that was breaking her heart in two? The only way she could say goodbye to Michael was if Cody were in real danger. Was he? She just didn't know.

She leaned back in the chair and thought about what Michael had said—not just his words, but his inflection. An inner warmth trickled through her. There was no use denying that she had hoped he would forgive her, yet now that the time had come to talk she felt strangely numb.

It had been as though she'd lived in a bubble these past few weeks, with all her energy having been spent on winning his trust and knocking herself out with the house. Adrenaline and a thin veneer of hope had kept her moving forward. She'd ignored a sense of foreboding whenever Robert entered her conscious thoughts and clung to the notion that a miracle really would happen.

Suddenly Nicole felt drained, every muscle in her body aching. Tonight there would be no pretending. Tonight there would only be truth.

She dragged herself off to the bathroom, stripped lethargically and stepped under the warm spray of the shower. There she stood until the water ran cold and then she got out and toweled off. She walked to the mattress on the floor—a new one that Michael had bought for her shortly after Cody's arrival—and lowered her listless body to it. Maybe a short nap would help. She would need all the strength she could muster to tell Michael about her past. And worse—about their hopeless future.

Slipping a knee-length nightshirt over her head, she spread out on the cool sheets and wondered what Michael would think when he learned what a mess she'd made of her life. He was basically too kind and understanding not to forgive her once he knew the whole truth. She could already imagine his hard body pressed against hers, his arms tightening around her, comforting her, his husky voice in her ear whispering reassuring words. With all her body and soul she ached for this and more, but she couldn't let it happen.

Depressed, she rolled over on her side. She had to find a way to explain there could be no future for them. Nothing permanent, anyway. All she could offer him was a day at a time. And even for her that wasn't enough.

Michael hung up the phone, his hand lingering on the receiver. He was being paranoid. Of course Nicole was safe. There had been no sign of a stranger lurking about all summer…and for who knows how long before that. Suddenly he wanted to know all about this woman who had wreaked havoc with his heart since the day he'd set eyes on her.

He let go of the phone and started to leave when he heard laughter coming from somewhere behind him. It sounded painfully familiar. He stood perfectly still and listened again. Barely able to breathe he heard his mother's voice grow closer.

Before he saw it was Molly, he saw Max holding her arm, and Michael's heart thudded harder in his chest.

Max stepped away from Molly and came closer, his hand ready to shake Michael's. "Michael! What a pleasant surprise."

Michael ignored the hand, stared from one smiling face to the other and then spun on his heel. "Thanks for the use of the phone," he said between clenched teeth and left.

He could hear Max dogging him all the way to the barn, where Billy was just leading a pony from a stall. Apparently seeing the storm heading his way, Billy kept moving. "Think I'll go show Cody his ride. Meet ya out back."

Michael shot him an accusing look as he passed, not knowing what to do next. With hands on hips and breathing hard, he spun around, ready to follow Billy. But Max stepped in front of him, blocking his path.

"Michael—"

Michael held up both hands, hoping to warn him off and hoping he would simply back away. Max didn't budge. "I should have knocked first. I had no business—"

"Michael, you're always welcome. You—"

"I should never have come."

"If we're going to be neighbors, we can't avoid each other forever. Why don't you come inside. We could sit down and talk."

"I have nothing to say."

"Oh, I think you do. You look like you'd like to punch my lights out. I think you have plenty to say."

"Nothing you want to hear."

"Try me."

Michael tried to pass again, but again Max stepped in front of him, and finally the last vestige of control slipped away. "Haven't you done enough already? First you seduce my mother—a happily married woman. Then you weave your magic on my sister, making her believe you're some kind of god. Now Molly, too?" He took an aggressive step closer and spoke between clenched teeth. "If you hurt my aunt, I swear you'll live to regret it."

A sheen settled over Max's eyes. He looked at one of the horses in the stall next to them and took his time responding. And when he did, his voice was low and ragged. "I would never hurt your aunt, Michael. It…it never occurred to me that my interest in her would affect you so." He looked down at his boots, then back up. "But I can see that it does…and I think I understand. I'll see to it that things are set straight.'' He turned to go, then looked back. ''I'm sorry, Michael…for everything.''

Michael had hoped Max would fight back, give him a reason to push him aside. But his contriteness had made that impossible. Michael watched the tall, lean frame—one so much like his own—walk away, and he bent his head.

Damn. Just when he thought he had things under control. Why did this man have to be with Molly?

And why did she have to look so happy? Of all the men in the world, why Max? A little voice kicked his conscience with a sarcastic retort. *Why not Max?* What was there not to like about the man? Except that he was the biological father that Michael's dad should have been.

Michael leaned against the gate of an empty stall, crossed his arms and lowered his head. He could still see the pain on his dad's face when the truth had come out, the pain so acute that it contorted his features and left him sobbing uncontrollably. Something had changed with that telling. Certainly not their love for each other. That could never change. Though they never spoke of it again, there was a sadness in his dad's eyes that never truly went away. Even though he had known the truth for years, it was as though as long as he kept it from his son it wasn't true. The truth had not set him free. It had broken his heart and condemned him to an early grave.

Michael felt old beyond his years as he straightened his back and inhaled deeply, fortifying himself for the long ride home with Cody. The boy had been through enough. He didn't need to see something else was wrong. Nor did Nicole. She already had enough on her plate, too.

He stood there a little longer, smelling the fresh, sweet hay and cool, dry earth, listening to the occasional snort of the occupants who must have sensed his unrest, and he thought about his sudden outburst of anger. How much of his pent-up anger had he displaced toward Nicole? Yes, she had deceived him, but her very life may have been at stake. She had good cause to be guarded.

He shook his head, disgusted with his own shortsightedness. All this old baggage where his mom and Max were concerned had overflowed, almost destroying anything good that could come of his relationship with Nicole.

Well, all that was about to change. He started for the exit. Tonight he would apologize. He only hoped he wasn't too late.

He left the barn feeling better and with a new sense of direction. A few more yards and he found Cody with Hannah and Billy behind the house.

"There ya are!" Hannah said, heisting her great bulk off the glider and waddling closer. "Got some fresh-baked chocolate chip cookies still coolin' on the racks. Told Cody and Billy to leave their mitts off till ya joined us. Come on in the house and rest a spell before ya head back."

Michael patted his middle. "Gotta watch the waistline. Nicole's been feeding me too good. The rest of you go ahead." He smiled broadly, but he could tell by Hannah's squinting eyes that she wasn't fooled for a second. He wondered if she had overheard all his shouting at Max.

She wagged her arm toward the side door. "Billy, take Cody in. Get 'im some milk, too. I'll wait out here with Michael." She ambled back to the glider and patted the seat next to her, fully expecting him to obey her command.

His smile was genuine this time as he sat beside her, though he wondered what was on her mind. He hoped it wasn't about Max. He had had enough for now. Later he would dust it off and look at it again. Already he knew he hadn't handled things well. And already he worried what Max would say to Molly.

"She's a good woman, ya know."

"Molly? Yes, she is."

Hannah slapped his knee. "Ya know very well I ain't

talkin 'bout Molly...though she's very nice, too.'' She crossed her arms under her ample chest and hummed a weary, "Hmm, hmm. You boys all alike. It could be right under yer noses and ya wouldn't know. How many pretty young single women ya see around—ones who can cook and work hard and good with the little ones? Hmm?''

"Hannah...'' He tried to warn her she was treading on private turf, but he had a feeling Hannah was selectively deaf and dumb.

Billy and Cody came out, the latter licking off a wide white mustache. "I brought you one, Mr.—Michael. In case you get hungry on the way home.''

"Thanks, Cody.'' A rumble of distant thunder carried across the valley and Michael eyed the clouds rolling closer. "We better get back before the rain.''

Hannah said, "Ain't gonna rain today. I checked my *Farmer's Almanac.* We got ourselves a long, dry summer, I'm afraid. Mighty dangerous, if ya ask me.'' She nudged Michael with an elbow. "But maybe ya better git, jes' in case.'' She thumped the Bible he'd seen her reading earlier. "I've been saying some mighty powerful prayers that that ol' almanac is wrong. And w'all know which book is more powerful now, don't we.'' She laughed a loud, raucous laugh that was infectious and drew Michael into a hug before he could stand.

He laughed along with her, feeling better than he thought possible, considering whose yard he was in. He bussed her on the cheek and then hurried Cody into the saddle of his borrowed palomino. Billy said he'd be over first thing in the morning to carry out the old carpet and start sanding floors.

Michael and Cody started down the path and Michael bit into the cookie before they had gone a hundred yards. Just minutes ago he was sure he would never come near this place again. Now that he had vented some of the anger that he'd held back for seven years, he wondered if perhaps he might have been wrong.

But for now he put thoughts of Max away and worried again about Nicole. Were she and Cody truly safe here? Something was niggling at the back of his mind as they rode closer to the ranch. Something he thought he overheard the old man say...

"Mama! Mama! Come see!" Cody bounded down the hall but came to an abrupt stop when he saw his mother lying on the mattress. He tiptoed to her side as Michael watched from the doorway. "Are you sick, Mama?"

Nicole sat up slowly and rubbed her eyes with her fists, groggy from sleep and more than a little disoriented. Was it morning already? She heard crickets and looked out the window to find dusk instead of dawn. Then she saw Michael in the doorway, and the pain of wanting more than she could have rushed back to her.

"No, sweetheart. I'm fine. Just a little tired. Go on in the kitchen and I'll be there as soon as I'm dressed." He skipped off, looking happier than she'd seen him since they'd left Denver. She watched Michael tousle Cody's hair when he passed. Then he leaned against the doorjamb and smiled a lazy smile.

"Don't get dressed on my account."

She cocked her head and eyed him, trying to decipher his meaning. Had the suggestive tone in his voice been real...or an extension of her dreams?

"It's still hot out. Might be more comfortable like you are."

"But this is my nightshirt." She sat cross-legged on the mattress, tugging the shirt under her knees.

He flashed her a smile. "It's okay. Really."

"Mom?" Cody yelled from the kitchen. "I'm hungry."

Michael held out a hand and Nicole took it, letting him tug her to her feet.

"Can't let the boy starve, now can we?"

Nicole padded barefoot down the hall behind Michael, trying not to admire his cocky swagger and knowing full well that he knew she was watching him.

This night wasn't starting off at all the way she'd planned.

Later Nicole read Cody a story and listened to his prayer for Grandma Mabel's bad hip, and then she tucked a sheet under his chin and kissed him good-night. Slipping into the bathroom, she brushed her teeth and ran a comb through her hair. A shiver of anticipation shot down her back. It had been a long time since she'd felt the warmth of Michael's smile. It felt so good for him not to act angry with her. Still, she must remember not to encourage him. Perhaps talk of her past would cool things off between them.

She left the bathroom rolling her eyes. Who was she kidding?

She found Michael on the porch swing and shut the door noiselessly behind her. Cody was a pretty sound sleeper, but tonight she didn't want anything to interrupt what had to be said. She sat sideways at the opposite end of the swing, tucking her legs beneath her. He turned and faced her, and although he seemed pleased to see her he made no effort to touch her, which made things a little easier.

"I'm sorry—" she started.

"I'm sorry—" he said at the same time. And then they laughed softly.

"I'm sorry I didn't tell you everything long before Cody showed up."

"And I'm sorry I didn't give you a chance to explain...and about the way I've treated you since."

She shook her head. "It's completely understandable."

She fell silent for a moment, struggling to find the right words to begin. "Michael, I...I made some pretty stupid mistakes when I was younger."

"Who didn't?" he asked, draping his arm across the back of the swing. "Take your time, Nicole. I'm not going anywhere."

If only she could say the same thing, she thought, hugging her knees to her chest. On a long sigh she started again. "I met Robert Campbell when I was seventeen. He was nineteen and already making good money. He had that James Dean look about him...you know, dark hair, pouty mouth. He wore a black leather jacket and drove a shiny new black Cadillac. All the girls thought he was cool. So when he asked me out I thought I'd won the lottery.

"My parents hated him at first sight. They didn't believe he could live on his own and afford all the toys he had and still be clean. He told me he ran a pharmaceutical cartel. He'd buy in bulk for various drugstores around town and warehouse the merchandise. He said he saved the stores a lot of money, that's how he earned his living.

"Eventually, when he started coming around all the time, my parents forbade me to see him. Of course that just added to the excitement. We sneaked around until I graduated and then we eloped.

"Dad was very strict and he hit the ceiling. He gave me an ultimatum—either come home and get an annulment or I would never be welcome in the house again."

Nicole looked at Michael, afraid to say what she was thinking, but knowing it would be unfair to stop short of the whole truth. "Michael...I thought he was on the up and up. I thought...well, I thought I was in love with him." Michael didn't even bat an eye. He just continued watching her, his look warm and caring.

"I got pregnant right away. That's when the real Robert started to surface. He wanted me to get an abortion. I wanted to make him happy, but I just couldn't do it.'' She looked down at her feet, ashamed at the next part. ''That's when he started knocking me around.

''I...I wanted to get away, but I was pregnant, no job, no employable skills, and I wasn't welcome back home. Besides, I kept thinking something would change.'' She gave a self-deprecating chuckle. ''Boy, did they change. I found out the drugstores weren't really stores at all. Then he got in a jam and went to a loan shark. When he couldn't pay the interest he just went crazy. That's when he held up a party store at gunpoint. He got caught within twenty-four hours and thrown in jail. Before he could make bail I found a shelter and left.

''I never saw him again. He didn't have to appear in court for the divorce, thank God. I tried to convince myself it was over. Yet something always bothered me. For some reason I thought he might come looking for us when he got out.

''Then earlier this year he wrote to me...said he wanted to see his son, that as soon as he was paroled and got his car out of storage, he'd be around to see us. That's when I had my last name changed to my mother's maiden name and left town.''

When she fell silent, Michael asked, ''Why your mother's maiden name?''

''If I used Keller—my maiden name—he would be sure to find me. I knew Robert didn't know my mother's name and...well, I hoped maybe my parents might try to find me someday and maybe check under that name. A long shot, I know. But I didn't know what else to do. After Cody was born I tried to reach them, but they had moved, and I couldn't find a listing for them anywhere around Denver.''

''Denver?''

''Yes.'' She raised her eyes but not her chin. ''I've never

been to Delaware. I'm sorry. It's just that at first I didn't—''

''It's okay, Nicole. I understand.'' He reached out finally and took her hand. ''Is that it?''

She tried and failed to ignore the impact of his touch and the longing it awakened. ''Isn't that enough?''

''Come here.'' He tugged her closer, and she found herself in his arms before she could think. ''You're a very brave young woman, Ms. Bedder, you know that?''

''Don't you mean very stupid?''

''No. I don't.'' They rocked gently without talking, listening to the crickets and the howl of a distant coyote.

She'd said it all, yet here she was, wrapped in the warmth of this good man's arms. She'd always known he would understand and forgive her. In many ways life would be easier if he hadn't. She could have left here knowing the decision had been his. But that wasn't Michael. Now it was up to her to back away and spell things out.

When he lifted her chin and gazed deeply into her eyes her brain told her it was time to move. Now. It was time to tell him she couldn't stay, that this would only make things more difficult. Her mind was sounding a loud alarm. But her body wouldn't listen.

Gently he kissed her, his lips warm and moist, his hands brushing her hair away from her face. She moaned into his mouth, knowing this was a mistake, but feeling powerless to do anything about it. She had to stop this. She…she…

She heard the scream from Cody's bedroom.

Eleven

"**S**tay here," Michael said, springing to his feet.

"I can't."

Cody cried out again, and Nicole followed Michael into the house. He stopped just outside Cody's door and held a finger to his lips. Then he pivoted quickly into the room, Nicole right behind him.

Cody sat in the middle of the bed, rubbing his eyes and sniffling.

Nicole raced to his side and took him into her arms. "Sweetheart, what is it?"

Between small hitches of breath, he said, "He was here. In my room."

"Who, Cody?" Michael said, looking around frantically.

"The bad man in the picture." Then he opened his eyes wide and looked around, seeming startled by the presence of Michael and his mother. "It was a really scary dream, Mom. He wanted to take me away, and I kicked him real hard. But he had a big gun and—"

"Shh. That's enough, young man. It was just a nightmare." She said it aloud...as much for herself as Cody. Perhaps it was his talk with Michael and Billy earlier that had triggered such thoughts. Whatever it was, her imagination had gotten the better of her, too. And by the looks of Michael, she would have to say he had been just as worried.

"Can I sleep with you, Mama? Just this once?"

Nicole looked at Michael, trying to gauge his reaction. She knew this wasn't how he'd thought the night would end. She also knew it was for the best. Her emotions had taken over; next time would be different.

"How would you like a piggy-back ride?" Michael said, offering his back next to Cody's bed.

Cody wrapped his legs around Michael's waist and put his arms around his neck, and Nicole followed them to her room. Michael tucked Cody under the covers and he was asleep within seconds. In the doorway Nicole started to apologize, but Michael put a finger to her lips, then kissed her on the nose.

"Sleep tight, my love. We have all the time in the world."

Sadly she watched him walk to his room and thought— if only that were true. If only that were true.

The next afternoon, when Nicole and Cody arrived home from the ranch, Billy was just walking out the front door, covered from head to toe in dust and wearing a red bandana over his nose and mouth.

Cody giggled and Nicole said, "You look like a stage coach robber out of an old Western."

Billy pulled the dusty red triangle down and started brushing himself off. "Good thing you weren't here today. What a mess! But I got it all done. Even cleaned up so it's ready for me to stain tomorrow," he said, looking physi-

cally spent but justifiably proud as he headed for his horse.
"Right now, though, a shower sounds pretty good. See you
two in the morning."

"Thanks, Billy."

Nicole waved goodbye and then sent Cody into the yard
to play until dinner. She needed some time alone with Michael. Something had happened today that he should know.
And if they didn't get interrupted she would tell him what
she had planned last night. As much as she hated the
thought of it, the anticipation had become almost as painful.

Inside she found him walking over the hardwood floor
inspecting Billy's work. He turned and smiled—that killer
smile that almost made her forget what she wanted to tell
him.

"Billy did a great job, didn't he?" Michael asked, his
eyes not leaving hers. "He even covered all the doorways
and stairs so that the dust didn't travel all over."

She held his gaze a little too long, her heart pounding
away again as it did every time he looked at her this way.
His mind was no longer on Billy and neither was hers. It
was as if they were back on the swing where they had left
off last night.

Quickly she glanced around for a place they could sit
and talk, only then remembering that all the furniture had
been moved out. The kitchen with its stone floor would still
be intact and the idea of a table between them suddenly
sounded easier.

"Do you have time for something to drink?" she asked.

"Sure. Just let me wash up."

"Lemonade, iced tea or beer?" she asked, heading for
the kitchen.

"Iced tea. Thanks."

Thanks was such a simple word, Nicole thought, pulling
a pitcher from the refrigerator. Yet it meant so much when
Michael used it. He never expected her to wait on him.

And even though cooking and cleaning was her payment for room and board, often he would help her in his unassuming way. If she searched all the world, where would she find a better man? Besides his innate goodness there were other things—his slow hands, his gentle touch, his desire to please. Nothing like Robert.

Robert. How had she been so blind? If she hadn't been so rebellious and impulsive, she could have had a real man, a man who far exceeded her best dreams.

If only—two of the saddest words.

Nicole washed and dried the table, removing the thin layer of dust that had seeped around the plastic door drop, and set her own problems aside long enough to think about Molly. Something was definitely wrong. It probably wasn't her business, but she knew Michael would want to know. She set out two glasses of ice, the pitcher and a plate of cookies, and she had just finished wiping down the countertops and cupboards when Michael rejoined her.

"Guess there was bound to be some dust in here. Our bedrooms and parlor are clean, though." He sat down and poured tea into both glasses and helped himself to a cookie. When she joined him he was slouched back in his chair and smiling at her again.

"So…what did you want to talk to me about?"

Nicole stalled for time by drinking some tea while she organized her thoughts. But when she set her glass down and looked back at Michael his smile had disappeared. He hunched forward and leaned his elbows on the table, giving her a sidelong look.

"What's wrong, Nicole?" There was a suspicion in his voice she didn't like. Where was this quick anger of his coming from? Why was it just below the surface, ready to pounce on the first available problem…or perceived problem, as was the case now?

"Michael—" She should just tell him the reason she'd

asked him to talk and not stray from her agenda, but she couldn't help it. She cared about this man. "Michael, you seem so angry. Like a time bomb ready to go off any second."

"Damn it, Nicole. That's not why we're sitting here. Don't play games with me. Tell me what's on your mind."

She was angry now, too, and she wasn't about to be bullied. She'd tell him in good time, but first things first. "There's a lot on my mind…if you'll just calm down."

He sat back, crossed his arms against his chest and ground his teeth, impatiently waiting for her to get on with it.

She sent up a quick prayer, hoping the bridge she was about to cross wouldn't be burned before she got to the other side. If her instincts were right, Max was at the crux of everything. If she had to leave here, at least she would leave knowing she had tried to help Michael work it out.

"Michael—" Why was this so hard?

He rolled his hand in front of him as if to say get on with it, which only provoked her and did nothing to help her find the right words.

"Okay. You want to know what's on my mind?" Already she didn't like her tone. This was coming out all wrong, yet it seemed fruitless to stop. "Max. What's your big hang-up with him? Why can't you stand to be around him?"

"And this is your business because—?" His sarcasm almost sent her over the edge.

"Because I—" She caught herself in time. There was no point telling him how she felt about him. Besides, at this very moment she wanted to go around the table and pound some sense into him. "Because *I* confided in *you*. I trusted you enough to tell you all about Robert. Why can't you tell me about Max?"

He pushed out of his chair and paced to the window. "It's...it's different."

She crossed to him quickly, not about to let him off the hook. "How is it different?" She tugged at his arm, forcing him to face her. His eyes were remote and they scared her. Yet she had gone too far to stop now. "Please. Tell me."

He tipped his head back and closed his eyes. A long and loud growl pushed through his slack mouth, straining the raised cords in his neck. When he looked back at her his eyes were a mix of anger and pain. And it looked as though she were about to pay the price for both.

"You want to know about your precious Max Malone?" He inched closer, his breath hot against her face. "He had an affair with my mother. Okay? You satisfied?"

She started to touch his arm but he shrugged her off. "Oh, Michael. I'm so—"

"Sorry?" He interrupted and sneered at her. "Sorry?" he said louder. "Yeah, well, so am I. Sorry I ever thought I could live near that man. Sorry I ever moved here."

"Michael, you don't mean that. You—"

"You don't know *what* I mean. You don't have a clue."

As much as she feared it, she knew the rest had to come out now or she would never have the nerve to broach the subject again—a subject that had obviously poisoned him with its silence.

"Then tell me the rest," she said softly, more worried than angry now. When he gave her his back instead of an answer she pressed harder. "Please, Michael. Maybe it will feel better if you just say it out loud."

He spun on her and grabbed her shoulders. "You think so? You think if I say out loud that Max is my father, that the man who raised me knew this, that carrying this secret and betrayal may have caused his early death, that the mother I thought was a saint never told me any of this before she died…you think saying it out loud will make it go away?'' He let her go roughly and turned.

Nicole stumbled backward, her heart in her throat. Michael stormed out of the house before she could recover. She stood right where he'd left her, her feet feeling as though they were mired in cement, her mind a jumble of facts and emotion that she couldn't sort out.

Finally she closed her eyes and prayed. *God, please help me do the right thing. I've opened up such a can of worms. Did you mean for me to do this? Did he really need to tell me?* In the quiet recesses of her soul, she thought she heard the answer.

Yes. As painful as it was. Yes, he did. And now maybe his healing could begin.

Slowly her breathing returned to normal, and she opened her eyes. She felt numb and vaguely nauseous, but at least her feet were willing to leave the spot she'd been riveted to.

She could see him leaning against a lone pine tree, his head hung low. More than anything she wanted to hold him close to her, to tell him how she felt. But knowing what lay ahead for them, she thought it wouldn't be wise, and that it wasn't what he really needed right now, anyway.

He needed a friend. And that she could be.

She slipped out the back door quietly, hoping he wouldn't run off. Whether he heard her approaching or not, she wasn't sure. At least he didn't move. She stopped next to him and followed his gaze to the mountains and the sun, now low in the sky above snow-crested peaks.

They stood there side by side without a word for the longest time. Words had simply failed her. There was nothing she could say that wouldn't sound trite. Therefore she said nothing, hoping her presence would somehow reassure him, comfort him.

After a while he slid down the tree and sat with his back

against the trunk. Nicole sat on the ground next to him, not too close, still afraid to look him in the eye. But even so she could feel that the rage had left him. In its place was a pain so palpable that it seared right through her, making her feel as if it were her own.

Slowly he lifted one arm from his lap. It hovered above the grass that separated them. Then he reached over, his palm up.

On a heavy sigh she took his hand and squeezed it. He squeezed back before tugging her closer. She went to him, knowing she shouldn't, but unable to tell him why. She laid her cheek against his chest as his arm circled her back. He rested his chin on her head, then kissed her hair ever so gently. Tears stung her cheeks and she wanted to brush them away, but she didn't dare move.

"I'm sorry, Nicole," he whispered into her hair. "I can be such a jerk sometimes."

She sat very still, wondering if she could escape this tender moment before it turned to more. She couldn't let him kiss her again without telling him she was leaving. Yet the timing was all wrong. He seemed so raw with pain.

"You were right. I owed you the truth," he said, still holding her close.

Slowly she eased herself away and started to speak, but he held a finger to her lips. With the back of his hand he wiped her cheeks dry.

"I was going to tell you. Maybe even last night...if things had worked out differently. It's just that you...well, it's no excuse, but you caught me off guard. I didn't see it coming." He tucked a stray lock of her hair behind an ear and eyed her evenly. "I've suspected for a while that my feelings about Max and my mom stood between us. I thought I could deal with it on my own, but obviously I haven't handled it very well. I'm sorry, Nicole. Am I forgiven?"

It was hard to find her voice, so she nodded and managed a weak smile. He pulled her back into his arms and rocked her, communicating more than words could ever say. She clung to him, wondering if she could ever feel closer to this man than she felt this very moment. He had shared something with her that she doubted he had ever said aloud. Perhaps not even to Taylor. And instead of staying angry with her, he was holding her close, assuring her she had done the right thing. *Oh, my love,* she thought. *If only things were different....*

"If I ever talk to you like that again you have permission to kick me where it hurts. Now," he said, setting her away from him a bit and smiling at long last. "What did you *really* want to tell me when you came home?"

Hesitantly she gazed up at his warm and expectant face and decided on the easier of her two subjects. "It's about Molly," she started. "I'm worried about her."

Michael's face suddenly reflected her own worry. "Is she sick?"

"No. At least I don't think so." She looked away, having trouble concentrating.

Michael touched her chin and turned her face back to him. "It's okay. Say anything. I promise." He made a big X on his chest. "I won't get angry again. No matter what."

Putting other thoughts away, Nicole let out a sigh and told him about Molly. "One of the little ones climbed up the stairs when we were all in the kitchen having a snack. The stairs lead to the guest room where Molly has been staying. I chased after him, and that's when I saw Molly's suitcases open on the bed. Her things were folded neatly inside…like she was getting ready to leave."

Michael frowned and she paused. He seemed to be thinking of something and she wondered if he knew why Molly might be leaving.

"And there's something else." She waited until she had

Michael's attention. "When I saw her first thing this morning her eyes were all puffy and red. I'm sure she'd been crying. And by the looks of her, I doubt she'd slept much, either."

She watched Michael hang his head and stare at the ground. He knew something. She waited, not wanting to pry it out of him.

Suddenly he sprang from the ground, brushed himself off and reached down for her hand. He gave her a tug and then squeezed her hand. "I'm going over to see Molly and fix this...if I can. I'll tell you all about it later, okay?"

Her curiosity could wait. She could see he was eager to get moving. "Okay. Well, then. Get moving."

She turned him toward the van, hoping he didn't see the pain on her face. Again the timing hadn't worked out, but sometime soon she would have to tell him that there could be nothing more between them—that someday soon she would have to leave.

With an exaggerated spring in his walk he called back to her. "I love it when you're bossy."

She forced a breezy tone. "Yeah? Well, it's a good thing."

She waited until he left and then she sat down in the grass and cried. When the tears subsided she got up and walked around to the other side of the house where she expected to find Cody. But he was nowhere in sight. She called to him. No answer.

The barn, she thought, wiping her face. He must be in there.

Twelve

Michael tore down the driveway and swung the van south onto the county road leading to the ranch, eager to have the experience over with so he could return to Nicole.

He'd rather have a tooth pulled without novocaine than face Max, but he had Molly to consider. If he had been the one to cause her pain, if he was the reason she was leaving—which he strongly suspected he was—then he had to make it right. If it meant going into Max's home and swallowing his pride, then that's exactly what he would do.

Max Malone. Amazing how one name conjured up such strong emotions, Michael thought as he drew closer. At the mere mention of the man's name he had unloaded his problems on Nicole. She had been right to confront him about an issue that could affect their lives, but simply telling her the facts had not changed how he felt about that man.

Still, there was one thing he couldn't deny. Malone blood pumped through his veins. It was a truth he wished he could deny—and usually did. He pulled to a slow stop next to the house and shut off the van. But for now he had to put all that aside and think only of Molly.

He was sitting behind the wheel, trying to corral his courage to enter Max's turf once again, when Billy exited the stable and rounded the front of the van. He came over and crossed his arms on the open window.

"What's up?"

"I came to see Molly. Do you know if she's around?"

"I'm sure she is. Want me to go get her?"

Billy was no fool. He had to know how uncomfortable it was for Michael to go inside.

"Thanks."

Billy slapped the side of the truck, spun around and was gone. A moment later Molly came out, her eyes as sad and swollen as Nicole had said.

Michael got out of the van and gave her a long hug. "Can we go for a walk? Do you have time before dinner?"

She smiled up at him. "I'll make time."

They sauntered along for some time without saying anything.

"Molly…you're planning to leave, aren't you?"

She nodded slowly. "Yes. First thing in the morning. I was going to stop by before I left…but I'm glad you're here now…that we have some time alone."

"It's because of me, isn't it?"

She kept looking ahead, her silence the only answer he needed. "If it's because of what I said to Max…please, you must tell me. I was way out of line."

She didn't say anything for a while as they kept walking. Then she glanced over at him. "I've had time to think about it and…Michael, I understand. I only wish I could say something that would make you think differently about Max. For your sake as well as mine."

"So do I," he said, surprised with his own response.

She looked at him hard now. "Really?"

"Yes, I do. But I can't imagine what you could say—"

"Will you give me a chance to try?"

He shrugged. It was the least he could do; he owed her.

She took his hand and led him up a long incline to the shade of a large maple where they sat in the grass. He sat cross-legged facing her and picked at a tall reed next to him.

"Michael, this may be painful for you to hear, but I think it might be time you did." She pulled her legs to her chest and rested her chin on one knee. "I'd like to tell you about your mother…some of the private talks we had over the years, especially during that difficult time before you were born."

Michael felt uncomfortable yet tried not to show it. The idea of his mother with Max… He had to shake the image before it could form. He had always known her as his mother, his dad's wife, a nurse, a good caring person who happened to be female. But thinking of her as a healthy, vibrant, passionate woman with needs not unlike his own…

He exhaled loudly and nodded for Molly to proceed.

"First, I want you to know that your mother loved John in her own way. He was a good, kind man and a terrific father, as you know.

"They were both young when they got married. And like so many young people, I don't think she knew who she was yet, what she wanted. Nursing was certainly important to her—she knew that. It gave her a place to pour out the passion she had in her." Molly glanced over at him and regarded him cautiously. "More than once she cried on my shoulder about one of her patients who didn't survive…maybe a young mother like herself…sometimes a child. Being a surgical nurse took its toll on her. I don't want to say anything negative about your father. I loved him, too, you know."

"I know," Michael said. "It's okay."

"John didn't want to hear about the hospital. If she cried about it, his answer was to quit the job. He made decent money. Somehow they'd manage. But that wasn't what she wanted to hear. She wanted to be held and comforted. And your dad wasn't much of a talker, either. So your mom felt lonely sometimes. She longed to share so much with him.

"Which brings us to Max. I'm not saying what they did was right, but I want you to know something. It was at least as painful for your mother and for Max. Not just the guilt—and believe me there was guilt—but after the closeness they experienced, well... I know you don't want to hear this, Michael, but they loved each other deeply. Yet your mother, your dear, sweet mother...she couldn't leave, she couldn't take Taylor away from John and move across the country...she just couldn't bring herself to hurt him like that.

"I was the only one she could tell the whole story to and trust that she wouldn't be judged. In fact, Michael, if I were to be completely honest with you, I should tell you that I thought she should go with Max. He was her soul mate. But she said no. She couldn't live with herself if she did.

"And so she stayed. And in doing so she lost so much of herself. She didn't know she was pregnant when Max left. And when she found out, she knew she could never tell him. It had hurt too much already. For both of them. When she told him she couldn't leave John, he accepted her decision. In fact, he said he even loved her more for it—for being the kind of person she was.

"There's something else you should know, Michael. This wasn't some sordid affair where they slinked around behind your father's back. This was a friendship that went on for years without so much as a kiss. Only once did it go further. That was a night when they lost a colleague on the table. Max was operating and your mom assisted. After, they were both very tired, both very sad, and their defenses were down. They made a mistake. Look what it cost them.''

Michael felt numb, not knowing what to think about this new information. He thought about his outburst with Nicole earlier and all the rage he had poured out to her. But anger no longer described the feelings churning around inside him. Confusion or frustration, perhaps. Not just for himself, but for both of his parents. And what about Max? Was it possible to feel sympathy for the man who he'd blamed for all this mess? In fact, how much blame could he lay at Max's feet? Certainly not all of it.

In the end it was the deception that Michael thought hurt him the most. ''Molly? Why didn't Mom tell me?''

''You were barely out of high school when she died. Had she lived longer, I'm sure she would have. But sweetheart, picture young Cody. If he were your son, could you tell him now?''

''No.''

''Or Billy? He's sixteen.''

''I don't know.'' Probably not. Teenage years were tricky enough.

''And think about it a moment, Michael. What if Cody really was yours as a result of one night, just one time when you got carried away? How would you feel if he avoided you like the plague? If he didn't want to be in the same room with you, if you couldn't touch him, hug him, or tell him how you felt?''

Cody wasn't his, but another child with Nicole could be—for all the protection they'd used. Yet he felt no guilt, no regret. Even if he had learned later that she was married, it would be hard to convince himself he'd made a mistake in loving her the way he had that night.

So who was he to judge?

Suddenly he realized just how self-righteous he had been,

how much more there was for him to consider, not the least of which was understanding and forgiveness.

Molly took Michael's hand. "I know how much you loved your father, but Michael…somewhere in the deep recesses of your heart, isn't there a part of you that would like to get to know Max better, to at least like him?"

He couldn't look Molly in the eye or she would know the truth…a truth he wasn't ready to admit to himself.

"Are you afraid of being disloyal to your father? Is that it?"

That was exactly how he felt. He nodded slowly.

"That's understandable, sweetheart. But your dad's gone and you can't hurt him now, not even his memory. He's engraved on your heart forever. It's possible for you to care about Max without changing how you feel about your dad. They're two separate and distinct relationships. I wish you'd give Max a chance, dear."

Michael looked away and toyed with another blade of grass, tearing it into tiny pieces until nothing was left, then he turned to his aunt. "You care about him a great deal, don't you?"

It was Molly's turn to look away. She looked down, her eyes brimming with unshed tears. "I could never hurt you, Michael. You've had enough pain in your young life—"

"But if you care about him—"

"I have to put you first. Just as your mother did."

Michael swallowed hard, feeling so selfish. Four people had put his needs first for nearly twenty-seven years. And he had almost let Nicole get away from him by judging her through his jaundiced eyes, mostly because of an attitude built on ignorance. That excuse would no longer fly.

"Molly, if you think you could have a future with Max, you have to stay and figure it out."

"I can't—"

"Please. I want you to." When she shot him a dubious

look he added, "It may take me a while to absorb all this, but I want you to be happy."

Molly swiped at her wet cheeks. "You sure?"

Michael smiled at her. "I'm sure." He moved closer and took her in his arms. "I'm sorry, Molly."

"You have nothing to be sorry about, sweetheart."

"Oh, yes, I do," he said on a long sigh. And then he stood. "Speaking of which…would you mind getting Max for me? I'd rather not go in there with everyone around."

"Gee, I'm sorry, sweetie, but he's not here. We thought I was leaving in the morning. We already said our good-byes. He's seeing a few patients at the hospital and spending the night there."

Maybe it was just as well, he thought. He could use some time. He wasn't sure he could do justice yet to what needed to be said. God knew that Max deserved an apology after the angry words that had been said, words that had caused him and Molly unnecessary grief.

As they walked back, Molly said, "I'd like to tell Max about our conversation."

"Of course. You can even tell him I feel like a jerk for the things I said."

Molly squeezed his hand. "He understands, sweetheart. Believe me, he understands."

Michael walked into the kitchen. He felt emotionally spent, and a melancholy mood began seeping through him. The table was set, and when Nicole spotted him she pulled a casserole from the oven and summoned Cody to the table.

He made awkward attempts at casual conversation throughout dinner, but it was all he could do to eat. Thankfully Cody filled in the long silences. He talked about his day with the Malone children and then later how he got into trouble for hiding in the barn and scaring his mother half to death.

Michael listened to the little guy and remembered all that Molly had said. He had a sudden urge to pull the boy onto his lap and let him know how important he had become to him. But he didn't, of course. Instead he stayed shrouded in the swirling fog of surrealism that had wrapped itself around him, one that had left him feeling isolated ever since he'd left the ranch.

After dinner, when Nicole shooed Cody into the other room, leaving them alone to clean up, Michael knew she was waiting to hear what had happened, yet he wasn't ready for more than a brief summary. He had a lot of thinking to do first. He knew how he *should* feel, what would make everyone happier, probably even himself, but old habits die hard. His anger toward Max had been his shield for so many years that the idea of shedding it made him feel naked, vulnerable.

"Max wasn't there," he said finally. Nicole stopped loading the dishwasher and looked at him. "But I talked to Molly and she's staying."

Nicole exhaled a sigh. "Oh, good. I'm so glad. She seemed happy here...until...well, recently." He knew she was waiting for him to volunteer more, but he couldn't. Not yet. Dinner, as well as emotions, sat heavily at the back of his throat.

"I was thinking of taking Mae out. Do you mind?"

"Are you okay?"

He nodded slowly. "I just need to think." When she looked worried, he touched her shoulder. "Not about us. About Max...and...and all that."

"Michael, we need to talk—"

"I know. And I'll tell you all about it. Soon, I promise. But if you don't mind, not tonight, okay?"

She lowered her eyes and resumed loading the dishwasher. "Okay."

He watched her a moment. He couldn't tell if she was relieved or disappointed.

"Should I wait up?" she asked, not looking up.

"I'm kind of bushed. Thinking of calling it an early night."

"Yeah. Me, too." She folded the dish towel and hung it over the handle to the oven. "Tomorrow I finish painting trim." She glanced at him briefly. "Maybe a little extra sleep will do us both good."

"Nicole, I—I'm sorry. But I really need some time alone tonight. I'll make it up to you," he said.

Her smile seemed forced, and he wondered if something else was bothering her. "It's okay, Michael. Really it is."

He hesitated a moment and then left the house, puzzled as to why she didn't seem happier tonight. He'd apologized for his earlier behavior, and he thought he'd handled the previous night's conversation about her past pretty well. He hadn't judged her or made her think her story upset him in the least. In fact, she had to know that if Cody hadn't had a nightmare, he would have made love to her.

He saddled Mae and walked her out of the barn, all the time wondering if he was making a mistake not staying with Nicole tonight. Why did she look so tense…as if she were conflicted about something? Could it be that she was questioning her feelings for him? After today's explosion and having been married to a man like Robert, who could blame her?

Maybe he'd just have to give her the space he was now asking for himself. He could do that. After all, just because they lived under the same roof didn't mean he should assume she wanted to make love with him at every turn. There hadn't even been talk of a commitment or the future.

He threw his leg over the saddle. Sometimes he could be pretty dense. He would take things a little slower and show her he was the man she hoped he was, the man she would want for a lifetime.

Thirteen

The week passed quickly, with Billy painting ceilings and Nicole finishing trim and making tremendous progress on the wallpaper. She worked long and hard hours, almost as if she were on a one-woman mission to complete the place in record time. Michael admired her stamina, but it left them zero time to talk. After a late dinner she would read to Cody and crash. If Michael didn't know better he would think she was avoiding him.

It was Saturday and he was replacing rotted boards on the exterior of the house in preparation for paint. Even though the hot sun was relentless, he liked working outside. It gave him time to think. About Max. About his dad. About his mom. And always about Nicole and Cody.

He hadn't talked with Max yet. And he hadn't repeated his conversation with Molly to Nicole, either. Thankfully, she hadn't pressed him. She had to know he would come to her when the time was right. And lately he thought that time was drawing near.

He could honestly say he was no longer angry with Max. What exactly he *did* feel was still a bit muddled, but it no longer felt like an open wound.

Late afternoon Michael put his tools away and found Nicole and Billy still at work. The three of them had been working seven days a week, and the house was shaping up nicely. He had just about convinced them to take the next day off when Nicole threw out a condition.

"Only if you'll go to church with Cody and me in the morning," she said, cocking her head at him in that challenging way of hers.

Strange, he thought. She'd never suggested that before. But why not? "Okay. It's a deal…but only if you promise to do nothing but relax all day." He wanted to add *and tell me what's bothering you* but Billy was still in earshot.

"Actually, I was thinking that maybe Cody and I would go visit Mabel. I talked to Walter yesterday and she's home from the hospital. Cody's just the medicine she needs right now."

They both waved goodbye to Billy and then Michael said, "I bet you're right." It was difficult not to show his disappointment. He had hoped they would spend the day together.

"Billy's been working on my car here and there. He says it should handle the trip just fine, so maybe we could drive separately to church."

"You sure? You could drive the van or I could take you to see Mabel."

"If I don't drive that old Chevy once in a while she's going to die on me. As for you going with me, thanks, but you'd be bored silly. There must be something else you could do."

Yes. There was. His apology to Max was long overdue. But again he wondered if Nicole was intentionally avoiding him.

* * *

In spite of Michael's misgivings they went to church the next morning in two separate cars. All of the Malones were there, including Max with Molly on his arm. It still felt awkward, but Michael made a valiant effort to be friendly.

After the service, while the family visited with other Joeville neighbors on the front steps, Molly pulled Michael into a bear hug and whispered, "I'd like to go back to Taylor's for a little visit. It would be nice if you would give Max a ride home."

Ah, now he understood. A conspiracy if he'd ever seen one. First Nicole made it clear she preferred seeing Mabel without him, now this with Molly. Regardless, the timing was right and the plan was set into motion. But when everyone got into cars to leave and no one gave a second look at Max leaving with Michael, he couldn't help but chuckle out loud.

"Are you thinking what I'm thinking?" Max asked, snickering as the last car left the parking lot.

"I'm afraid so."

Side by side they sat in the idling van, silence stretching between them.

"There's a pretty view of town and the steeple across the valley up there." Max pointed to a southeastern ridge. "It's one of Josh's favorite spots. He and Taylor go there sometimes. It's a...quiet place to talk...uninterrupted."

Michael put the van in gear and drove in the direction of the ridge. An apology wouldn't take that long; it was the rest of it that had his gut in knots. Would he find the right words? Could he truly make peace with this...this good man?

Words from this morning's sermon trickled back. *Who will cast the first stone?* And Michael knew what had to be done. Of course he could make peace. It was simply a decision—one he embraced wholeheartedly.

He shifted into low and the van strained up the steep incline until they reached level ground and the magnificent view Max had promised. When Michael turned off the engine and they stepped from the van, the sound of grasshoppers rose to a higher pitch.

Max was no sooner propped on a boulder than Michael began, eager to have the first part over with. "About that day in the barn—" Max held up a hand to stop him, but Michael persisted. "I was way out of line. I'm sorry."

"Apology accepted."

"Molly told you—?"

"Everything. Yes."

Michael heaved a sigh and found a rock of his own facing Max. Now what? What did a guy say to a man who was his father and a stranger?

Max must have sensed his uncertainty. "Michael…I realize John was your real father—the man who raised and loved you. He should always be thought of that way. Believe me. I understand this completely."

Michael saw a distant hurt in Max's eyes that didn't seem to have anything to do with the moment.

"Maybe it would help if I explained something." Max took a deep breath before he proceeded. "This is no longer a secret, and I've checked with Shane. He doesn't mind that we discuss this."

"Shane? I don't understand."

"First, I want you to know I asked Taylor not to say anything until we thought the time was right and then I would tell you. And second, I don't want you to think that what I'm about to tell you is an excuse for the wrongs I've done."

"Okay," Michael said, more confused than ever.

"Do you mind if I start from the beginning?"

"Please do."

Max exhaled loudly before he began. "My wife was an

only child, the daughter of a wealthy Denver industrialist and his socialite wife. I don't think Christina had an inkling as to what Montana ranch life would be like. I did my best to explain how desolate it can seem to someone used to an active social life, but she assured me that it sounded very romantic. In truth—and I know this isn't kind—but I think the only thing that sounded romantic to her was the fact that I was a surgeon.

"Anyway, for my first rotation at U of M Hospital in Michigan I had wanted her to go with me, but she had already become disillusioned with life as a doctor's wife, so she remained here. That's when she had her first affair. How many more there were, I'm not sure, nor did I ask. The truth of the first one had left such a scar that I didn't want to know more."

Max paused, his face stricken. Then he waved a hand. "I'm sorry. I'm drifting. The most important part for you to know is that a year or so before your first visit here, Shane learned that I wasn't his...that I wasn't his biological father."

Michael didn't know what to say. The subject was quite obviously still painful. And then a question did come to mind. "Did you know all along?"

Max nodded. "From very early on, yes."

"Before you and Mom—?"

"Yes." Max eyed Michael evenly. "But what happened with your mom was not payback or something to salve my bruised ego. You must believe that." He leaned his elbows on his knees and stared at the ground. "Besides, Christina was gone by then. Suicide, I'm sorry to say. Another thing I will forever feel responsible for."

"But why would you—?"

"I should have realized from the get-go that she was too fragile for this kind of life. I could have sold the ranch and practiced medicine in Denver so she could have remained near family and friends.''

"But someone told me the ranch has been in your family for four generations. You couldn't have just sold it to strangers.''

Max looked up and smiled. "Fifth generation soon. I'm glad you understand how I could feel about this place.''

"Heck, I haven't lived at my place a year and already I'm having a hard time with the prospect of selling her.'' It was true, though he hadn't said it out loud before. Ever since he and Nicole... He shook his head and refocused on Max.

"Look, Michael. I know you will always think of John as your real father, but maybe over time we could have something else. I don't know what to call it. Friendship maybe? It feels so—''

"Strange?''

"Yes, I guess.'' He stood as if to leave, but then he hesitated. "For now, do you think you could...forgive me?''

Michael watched Max's arms hanging straight at his sides and waited for them to move, for his hands to reach out. Michael sensed Max wanted to, but he didn't, which left Michael strangely disappointed.

"Of course,'' Michael said, hearing the coarseness in his own voice. But in his heart he knew things had already progressed beyond forgiveness.

When they got back to the ranch another milestone was reached. Max invited Michael in for lunch and he accepted. Now he wished Nicole and Cody were here to share this moment. While he still felt a little ill at ease in Max's home, it had nothing to do with the way he was treated. Even if he hadn't had a drop of Malone blood in him he suspected he would have been treated just as well. These were truly good people, and whether he thought of them as family or neighbors, it didn't matter. They were very special either way.

Billy passed a plate of brownies and asked Michael, "When do you think you'll be ready for exterior painting?"

"Oh, a few more days, I imagine."

Ryder said, "I don't plan to work next Saturday, if you'd like an extra hand."

Shane said, "Same goes for me."

"Me, too," said Josh.

"I could make the meals," Jenny added.

"I could watch the kids," Hannah said.

Max, Molly, Taylor and Savannah threw their hats in, too.

"Cool," said Billy. "It can be like an old-fashioned barn-raising Grandpa used to tell me about…except the barn is already raised. All we have to do is paint."

Max joined in. "I bet we could get the whole job done in one day if we start early and the weather cooperates. Besides, I'd love to see the old place and what you've done with her." He eyed Michael, leaving no doubt in Michael's mind that the offer had come from the heart, not out of some sense of obligation. He was truly touched.

"I don't know what to say. It would take me ages to do it alone." He glanced around the room at the smiling faces. "I accept! Saturday it is."

A big cheer went up and then there was the loud buzz of plans being made—equipment needed, menu ideas, how to occupy the children.

Yes, indeed, Michael thought. He was one lucky guy.

Nicole pulled up the drive and let out a relieved sigh. She was glad to see Michael's van alone in the drive. A day of peering around corners for a black Cadillac had left her nerves frazzled. After months of lulling herself into a false sense of security, recent talk of Robert, along with Cody's nightmares, had awakened a sleeping dragon. Now she imagined him lurking around every corner. Taking Cody into town with her suddenly seemed very risky.

She stepped from her car and a heavy sadness returned. The house would be done soon and she would be out of excuses. If only there was a way she could stay here forever. But what if Robert found them and the courts allowed visitation? She couldn't bear the thought of Cody spending one second with that animal.

Michael walked out onto the porch and she forced her glum mood aside. She was home, temporary as it was. And for the time being she and Cody were safe.

She watched Michael moving closer and she wanted to cry. How much longer could she keep her distance from this man who meant the world to her, whom she ached to hold close and never let go?

Cody jumped out and ran around the front of the car. "Can I go see the horses, Mama?"

"Sure, big guy." She watched him run off toward the barn, not a care in the world. What would leaving here do to him?

"How's Mabel?" Michael asked, taking her hand and leading her to the porch swing.

"Much better." She sat down next to him, trying not to enjoy his touch quite so much and noticing something behind his smile. "How was your day?"

"Oh, I'd say it went at least as well as all of you planned." He squeezed her hand.

There was no point pretending she and the others hadn't talked and hoped he and Max would get together, so she didn't try. "Want to tell me about it?"

"Later. After Cody goes to bed."

It would be much easier now in the light of day, but she couldn't say that. Instead she said, "Okay."

"Want to guess what's happening Saturday? Or do you already know that, too?"

She told him she didn't, so he filled her in on the group's plan to paint the exterior, but she only heard half of what he said; her mind and heart were focused on the strong yet gentle feel of his fingers on hers. Still holding her hand he led her off the porch, turned and studied the house. She pretended to swat an invisible insect and gently withdrew her hand from his.

Michael looked up at the roof. "Good thing for the pocketbook that the roof was replaced a few years ago, except now I'm stuck with the color. Where on earth did they find shingles with purple flecks?"

She swallowed the lump in her throat. "I kind of like it. Old Victorians are called Painted Ladies for a reason, you know."

"But what colors would go with it? I certainly don't want to keep it pink."

"I've been thinking about that," she said, happy for a neutral subject.

"Why does that surprise me?"

God, how she loved his smile. "How about a light gray on the siding with white trim on the gutters, windows, porch and then a real deep plum on the shutters and a few other places. Just enough so you could call it the Purple Palace Inn."

She watched him thinking and nodding, then he pulled her to him and kissed her forehead. It all happened so fast.

"What if you hadn't come along? How would I ever have pulled this off without you?"

She smiled into his chest, determined to sound normal. "Oh, I'd say you probably would have lost your entire life's savings and fallen flat on your face."

He laughed and gave her a squeeze. "And you'd probably be right." They walked inside hand in hand, then Michael took a pitcher of lemonade from the refrigerator. Lifting it toward her, she nodded and he poured two glasses, finally letting go of her.

"I suppose you have ideas for carpet, too."

She sat opposite him, missing his touch. "Well, yes. I thought—"

"Whatever you want is fine with me. Go ahead and order it. In fact, maybe you ought to do that this week so that it will be here about the time the wallpaper is done."

Nicole set her glass down and forced a weak smile. "Something I forgot to tell you. I'm good but I'm not fast."

He flashed her a wicked grin. "I know. Just the way I like it."

Nicole groaned inwardly and drank her lemonade. How much longer could she live under the same roof with this man and not go crazy with longing, a need so great it threatened to consume her? Not even the long days of physical labor had blocked out the steamy nights of fantasies and dreams. She finished her drink and poured a second one.

After Cody was asleep, Nicole slipped out onto the porch, a place that had once been their haven at day's end, a place they had shared dreams and secrets. She'd avoided this place for over a week now, but tonight she wondered if she should tell him of her decision. Eventually she would be forced to, yet she dreaded shattering their peaceful little world.

Maybe it could wait until after Saturday. After the painting was done and all of the Malones left. Yes. He was looking forward to that day. She didn't want to spoil it. She could wait a little longer.

There was a gentle breeze, warning of cooler nights to come, and nonchalantly Michael slid closer on the swing and wrapped his arm around Nicole. Without preamble he told her of his conversation with Molly about his mother and then today's meeting with Max. Michael explained he had needed time to sort out his feelings for Max and his mother so that he could feel whole, unencumbered by his past before starting a future…with anyone.

Nicole heard the implication and she understood all too well about resolving old issues. But no matter how much she wanted it so, she couldn't tell him what she knew he wanted to hear—that her past was now behind her, too. As long as Robert was out there somewhere, her future seemed so precarious. If he got as close as Joeville and she found out, she'd have to run and never return.

The very thought of it made her feel ill. Not just the fear of what Robert might do to her or Cody, but the prospect of leaving Michael. She'd been living a day at a time and doing her best to appreciate every minute. But she knew this wasn't enough for Michael. He deserved so much more. She was running out of time. Soon he would ask for a commitment she couldn't make.

Finally, when she said she was tired and excused herself, she saw the disappointment in his eyes. She didn't want to imagine what she would see when she said goodbye.

As the week progressed Michael had plenty of time to think as he caulked around the exteriors of windows and repaired shutters and the foundation of the porch—all in preparation for Saturday's painting. Something was bothering Nicole and he thought he knew what it was.

The chip he'd been carrying on his shoulder about women—because of his mom's relationship with Max and his bad experience with Roxanne—had manifested itself in more than one angry outburst. Nicole had to be leery as to whether these issues were finally resolved and behind him. With so much time working alone the past few days Michael was sure they finally were. Roxanne and Nicole were two entirely different women, and while he could never say he endorsed what Max and his mom had done, he could now say he understood and empathized.

And this made all the difference in the world.

Michael thought about how he would explain all this to Nicole, but by Thursday he had decided that there was one more thing he could do to convince her all was well and to make her truly happy. It would mean enlisting Josh's help and waiting a day or two more to talk to Nicole, but with any luck he knew the wait would be worth it.

Fourteen

On Saturday the heat was unrelenting with only an occasional cloud drifting overhead. Everyone worked at peak efficiency, surprising even themselves when the first prime coat of paint was finished before lunch.

Hannah kept the children busy and out of harm's way as the afternoon raced by and the finish colors came to life. Thunder could be heard in the distance, but the paint was drying quickly and still not a drop of rain had been felt.

At sunset, with the job finished, Billy and Ryder returned from Joeville with boxes of pizza stacked in their arms. Everyone was so hungry it didn't matter that it was no longer hot. Slices disappeared along with the salad Jenny had tossed together and the breadsticks Hannah had baked. They sat outside watching the orange sun paint the big sky behind the growing mass of gray clouds while they polished off most of the pizza. Some of the family sprawled out on the grass in front of the porch; others sat on the steps.

Higher up, Max, Molly and Hannah reclined more comfortably in highback wicker chairs.

Even the children seemed subdued, Nicole noticed, thinking their afternoon outside in the sun had tired them almost as much as the adults. Except for a few "mmmm-hmms" and "this is great" the conversation was sparse.

All day Nicole had felt the warmth and camaraderie of the Malones. Off and on she'd caught glimpses of Michael, and she knew he had finally made peace with Max. In time she thought he might even admit he felt proud to be part of such a loving family. At least he would have this when she was gone. What would she have but a broken heart. And Cody, of course.

The rare moment of envy disturbed her. Yet Michael had two families who cared; she wondered if her own had forgotten her completely. If they had, there was no one to blame but herself. She was the one who had defied them, who had gotten into trouble and run away. Being a mother herself now, she could only imagine the pain she must have caused her own mother.

Nicole shifted uncomfortably on the step, leaned her back against the porch railing and looked up at Hannah. She was staring at the sky and shaking her head.

"Don't look good," Hannah said. "God knows we need the rain, but what about all this new paint?"

Max, who sat between her and Molly, reached over and patted Hannah's knee. "The paint's been dry for hours now. A little rain won't hurt the house."

"I s'pose yer right, Maxwell, but somethin' in my bones ain't right. I've set my mind to worryin', and there's no convincin' me otherwise."

Max winked at Nicole, and she smiled.

"Okay, you young folks laugh at me. But mark my words. These ol' bones never lie."

Molly stood first and started gathering paper plates and

napkins, and soon everyone was stirring, carrying everything inside as thunder started rolling across the valley.

Josh took Hannah's elbow and helped her up. "I hope you're right about the rain." He looked up at the darkening sky. "My wheat could sure use it."

As soon as leftovers were put away, ice cream was dished out, and Nicole felt a surge of new energy from the sugar, as did the children who sat around the large kitchen table, giggling and enjoying each other's company. Cody was the only non-Malone offspring, but one would never know it. They had all taken him in and treated him as if he'd been with them since birth.

Nicole warmed at the sight of him with his new friends, and even though they couldn't stay she thanked God for sending them here. Of all the ads she could have answered, surely none could have paid so richly. She still didn't have much money to call her own, but if she didn't know it before, she knew it now—wealth could be measured in more important ways than money. And here she had found them all—friendship, love, a sense of belonging, a place she could give as well as get, a place she could feel safe.

Strange, but she hadn't thought of Robert at all today. Could all her recent anxiety about him have been in vain? Even if the stranger up north had been Robert, it seemed that if he had learned anything he would have shown up by now. Was it possible she and Cody could stay here, after all? She hugged herself and closed her eyes. This vacillating was driving her crazy. If only she knew the right answer. She knew what she wanted, but that didn't mean it was right.

She turned and opened her eyes in time to see Michael making his way to her side, licking the last of the ice cream from his spoon.

"Do you believe we got it all done? In one day?" He shook his head in astonishment and set his bowl on the counter behind him. "I've made the rounds and thanked everyone, but it hardly seems enough."

Nicole smiled up at him. "It's enough."

He looked at her, his gaze traveling from her eyes to her lips. He inched closer, and she knew he was about to kiss her. She closed her—

"Oh, no!" Hannah staggered to her feet, her hand clasped tight against her mouth, eyes wide. She pointed a shaky finger toward the front picture window. "Look."

Nicole saw the orange glow and sucked in a sharp breath. The sun had gone down some time ago. As hard as she tried to deny it, there could only be one explanation for what she was seeing.

Ryder ran to the phone and started punching in numbers, then stopped and eyed Michael, as if having second thoughts about taking charge. Michael waved his hand at the phone.

"Please. Go on. I wouldn't know where to begin."

Ryder finished dialing. "Whitey? Ryder Malone here. I'm at the old Palace and there's a fire headed this way." He listened intently as everyone looked on. "Great. We'll be on the lookout." He hung up.

"Someone already spotted it. Two tankers are on the way."

Michael raked his hand through his hair. "Will that be enough?"

"That's all they got." Ryder laid a hand on his shoulder. "Not to worry, little brother. We know what to do."

Michael stared into Ryder's dark eyes. No one had called him brother before. He thought it was no coincidence that Ryder chose this moment. It was as if he were saying "you're family and we'll protect you." How they were supposed to do that he wasn't sure, but he was sure that every person in this room cared as much as he did about his home, and the power of that was nearly overwhelming.

Josh stepped closer. "I'll take the plane up and check out the scope and direction of the fire. Keep your radio on."

"Good idea," Shane said. "Billy, come with me. We'll go roust the ranch hands and round up the equipment. Then we'll line up along the road south of the ranch with our lights on and wait to hear from you."

Josh nodded and took off out the door. Shane started to follow, then stopped and faced Ryder, who was right on his heels. "I'll run the plow crew. You want to organize the feeder trucks?"

"Sure. We'll get a back burn going."

Michael felt useless, standing there watching the others, all so knowledgeable and self-assured. He rushed to the door. "What can I do? Give me a job. Anything."

Shane motioned to Ryder as he ran out the door. "Go with Ryder. He'll need your help setting the fires."

Michael caught Ryder's arm before he could leave the house. "What about the women? The children? Will they be safe here?" Michael met Nicole's frightened eyes before he glanced out the window. The fire, still miles away, was definitely moving closer.

Max stepped into the circle. "They'll be safe here...at least until I get back. I'll know when to evacuate if need be."

"Back from where?" Ryder asked, sounding distressed.

"The ranch. I'll run over and get some medical supplies. Just in case. It won't take long."

"I don't know, Dad. The wind could change. I wouldn't want you trapped alone on the wrong side of the fire."

Max brushed by Ryder and Michael and walked out the door, calling over his shoulder. "Twenty minutes. Tops. Now go on. Do your job. I'll do mine."

Nicole raced to Michael's side. "Go. We'll be okay. Just tell me what we can do here."

If he had any doubts about his feelings for this woman, they all vanished in a heartbeat. If anything ever happened to her and Cody... He looked around at the worried faces of the women and children. "Think you guys can handle things here alone?"

Hannah pushed past Jenny and planted both hands on her hips. "'Course we can. We might be women, but we ain't weak, you know. I'll watch the young'uns whiles Jenny, Savannah, Nicole and your sister batten down the hatches. We'll be jes' fine. Now scat!"

Michael smiled, then whispered into Nicole's ear as he hugged her goodbye. "If it gets too close, let Mae out of the barn."

He stepped back, shot Nicole one last look, then ran after Ryder. He hopped into the passenger side of the truck seconds before it tore down the drive.

Nicole marshaled the women into action, gathering and covering all the paint supplies out in the field, then dousing them with buckets of water. Once that was finished she found extra lengths of hose in the barn and they strung all they could find into one long snake, first watering the barn, then moving to the roof of the house.

While Savannah and Taylor helped her maneuver the unwieldy hose, Jenny set up a tripod and camera and started shooting photos of the work and the distant fire. They all found it strangely beautiful in its volcanic brilliant colors, although never far from their minds was the fear and total devastation it could wreak if not controlled.

They were just finishing the roof when a single tanker roared up the drive. "Howdy, ma'am," the driver yelled from his open window. "I see ya got the roof already."

Nicole dropped the hose and ran to the truck, hearing

Jenny's camera clicking away. "I thought there were supposed to be two."

"There are," he said, removing his hat and dragging a sleeve across his forehead. "We saw the string of lights heading down the road. The other tanker's joining them."

"I'm sorry," Nicole said, remembering her manners. "I'm Nicole."

He settled his hat back on his head. "I'm Whitey. I head up the Joeville volunteer firefighters." He looked over his shoulder at the fire, then at the house again. "Think I'll wet down a few acres between here and there. Then I'll go refill at the pond in front of the Malone ranch. You know if anyone's over there to help me?"

"You might catch Max if you hurry."

Molly ran up. "Maybe you could wet down the ranch, too?"

He gave her an understanding nod. "Will do, ma'am. Now, all of you ladies just stay put and don't go near the fire. We'll handle it." He tipped his hat to Molly and Nicole and added, "Don't worry."

But Nicole did worry, as she was sure all the other women did. Their men were at risk.

Finally Nicole watched the red taillights dim when the tanker drove off and turned south on the county road. She thought Whitey had seemed calm enough. Was he that sure the fire could be contained? Or was he simply shielding them from a more devastating truth? Either way, there was nothing else left they could do but wait and pray.

She pictured Michael's strong face, and now she wished she had told him how she truly felt before he'd left. She wanted him to know she had never loved like this before, that she never would again. The gruesome thought that she might never get another chance to tell him crossed her mind, and she shuddered.

* * *

Michael gripped the armrest of Ryder's pickup as they tore around another bend in the road just south of the ranch. "What do you think, Ryder? You've seen this before?"

"Not since I was a kid...and not this close."

"But we *can* stop it, right?"

Ryder ducked his head for another look out the window. "I sure as hell hope so."

So did Michael. The image of Nicole's frightened face burned in his imagination. If only he could have stayed with her, made sure she was safe. Now he wished he hadn't waited to tell her how much he loved her, how he wanted to spend the rest of his life with her. He swallowed the bile rising in his throat, telling himself there would still be time. *God, please. Give us time.*

They followed Shane's Explorer up the last hill. Both vehicles skidded to a halt in the gravel outside the bunkhouse.

Michael heard the confidence in Shane's and Ryder's voices as they organized workers and barked out staccato orders, and he felt a measure of relief. Finally, they barreled down the county highway that cut diagonally between the ranch and the Palace. And there they waited, lights blazing, for Josh to pass over and give them directions.

Cold sweat ran down Michael's back as thunder rolled on, more furious and frequent. Lightning streaked the smoky black sky. The ferocious red line moved closer. Still no rain. The crack of timber sounded in the distance. Finally, Michael heard the drone of Josh's plane overhead, and Shane's two-way radio crackled a second later. "Swing the line to the southwest about fifteen degrees and I think you'll have it."

Shane gave the order and the engines revved. Ash already cluttered the air around them, and waves of heat carried the pungent scent of burning leaves across the once verdant valley. The tanker mopped-up, spraying hot embers wherever they ignited.

Michael wiped the sweat from his face and wondered how long before they'd have to retreat. Again he longed to hold Nicole, to assure her and himself that she would remain safe.

But the magnitude of what he and the crew were able to accomplish in the minutes ahead did much to assuage Michael's fears. Tractors plowed dry earth in wide swaths along the natural barrier of the road, bringing up moist soil. West of the road Michael rode on the tailgate of one truck spreading napalm. Soon he was on foot with the others, working in parallel lines, torching the dry earth in a back burn that stretched away from the Palace and toward the fast approaching fire line.

Even though the plan seemed a sound one, Michael kept an eye on the insatiable appetite and impatient fury racing down on them. It had devoured the last patch of forest in front of them and was gobbling up dry grass at an incredible speed. Finally Shane shouted the order to move out and everyone scrambled. He pulled alongside Ryder's truck and shouted over the roar. "Did you see Dad pass by?"

"Oh, no!" Ryder pounded the steering wheel and swore.

Without warning, the winds began eddying in tornado-like fashion, and a light rain began to fall. The fire line was shifting before it reached the backburn. And it was heading straight for the ranch. Shane barked orders to the crew as trucks raced a short distance ahead of the fire line. Their only hope was to go around it and pray they weren't too late.

Michael strapped himself into Ryder's pickup and held on tight as they bounced along the uneven ground, racing ahead of the slower moving heavy equipment. He didn't have to look at Ryder to know the panic he must be feeling, for he felt it himself. He'd had barely a second to celebrate Nicole's safety when he realized Max was in grave danger.

Flames to the right were greedily eating up acres of wild-flowers and tall grass on their relentless pursuit of the dense island of evergreens, birch and aspen that backed up to one corner of the ranch. Michael remembered seeing tree forts there and wondered if they were the children's new crea-tions or perhaps left over from earlier days, from his... brothers.

Brothers. Yes, they were. Only yesterday he would have denied it. But not anymore. And because of all they had done to protect his property, they now stood to lose some-one who was most dear to them—their father. His father.

Michael closed his eyes, heat and smoke burning his nos-trils as he inhaled deeply and prayed as he had never prayed before.

Fifteen

And then came the rain, no longer a light shower, but buckets and buckets of heaven-sent rain. The splitting and thud of falling trees slowed; the deafening roar of hungry flames now a whisper.

Finally Michael thought he saw something just ahead, through the beating of the windshield wipers. A roof? Could it be? Ryder must have seen it, too.

"Yes! Yes!" He didn't let up on the accelerator.

Then, through the storm, they saw the ranch, and they both let out a loud whoop.

But when they skidded to a stop behind Shane's Explorer, only the cracking of smoldering trees greeted them. The one thing they had prayed for was nowhere in sight.

"He has to be here somewhere. He has to."

The desperation in Ryder's voice echoed Michael's own feelings. Michael leaned his head back on the seat and closed his eyes, bile rising in his throat. Fear of what he might find kept his hand gripped to the door handle, his body motionless.

When he opened his eyes he saw the second tanker, driving slowly from the fire break. Whitey stopped the truck. Out stepped Max from the passenger side, round-shouldered and black from head to foot.

Michael let out a loud breath as Ryder jumped from the pickup and ran to embrace his father, Shane beating him to it.

Michael sat frozen in his seat, a mix of fear and other emotions leaving him dazed. Through the heavy rain he watched and waited, not knowing why until Max lifted his head. Then their eyes locked on each other and held.

And in the space of a heartbeat Michael realized how far he had progressed beyond forgiveness and acceptance. Max was no longer simply a good man; he was another father who had found a place in Michael's heart.

Back at the Palace a reporter and cameraman had just arrived and were talking with Jenny as the parade of vehicles drove slowly up the long drive. One by one the weary brothers stepped out and the women rushed to them, ignoring their blackened faces as they pulled them close, kissing them and crying tears of joy. The cameraman took a few photos of the happy reunion as Nicole ducked inside and away from the clicking lens. Michael gave her a knowing look and followed.

As soon as the news van left, Ryder, Shane and Joshua carried their sleeping children out of the house, leaving only Cody undisturbed. Michael held Nicole at his side as they waved their goodbyes. She had always felt good in the crook of his arm, but never as good as now. If anything had happened to her...

But it hadn't. She was safe. They all were, and for that

he was too grateful for words. Even the house had been spared.

Michael ran his hand over the porch railing beside them, his fingers coming away with nothing but water. The paint had held, and most of the soot had been washed away. He'd been lucky tonight. Damn lucky.

"You know, I didn't realize how much this place had come to mean to me until I almost lost her." He could say the same about Nicole, but soon he would show her just how very much she meant to him. And tomorrow, finally tomorrow, he would tell her all that had happened this week and ask her the question he'd been dying to ask. But for now, exhausted and emotionally drained, he simply smiled down at her and said, "After all this, I can't imagine selling it to strangers, can you?"

Nicole looked up at him, her eyes bright with rain and moonlight. "No, I can't. You've worked so hard—"

"*We* have." He interrupted. "You've been here every step of the way." He let out a long sigh, the reality of his decision starting to sink in. "But if I keep her, things will be pretty lean...maybe for a long time."

He expected her to say something, but when she didn't he tugged at her waist. "Come here, you," he whispered, his voice raspy, throat parched. She snuggled, but he said, "Closer."

She looked up at him, hesitant, maybe confused.

He lifted her up. "Wrap your legs around my waist. I want to feel your heart beating against my chest. I want to hold you until my arms can't take any more." He carried her that way into the house, surprised he had the energy.

"Michael," she said, her breath warm on his neck, "I'm dirty and sweaty."

He chuckled above her hair, knowing he was black from head to toe and must smell like a hundred overflowing ashtrays. "We'll have to do something about that, then, won't we?"

"You don't mean…?" She looked over her shoulder as they turned into the bathroom. "But, Michael—"

"Thank God you weren't hurt," he whispered. "I don't know what I would have done if—"

"I know," she said. "Me, too. But, Michael, we shouldn't—"

"Make love?" He didn't understand her hesitation. Tonight of all nights. "Look me in the eye and tell me you don't want to."

She started to look away and he turned her face to his. "Nicole…tell me. If you don't want me, I'll never force myself on you."

Her eyes looked confused and sad, her voice barely a whisper. "Oh, Michael…I do want you, but—"

"But nothing, my love. We can talk later. Right now let me love you." Hesitantly she reached up and wrapped her arms around his neck, and when his mouth met hers she kissed him long and hard as if never wanting to let him go.

He stripped her clothes from her and tossed them on the bathroom floor, his own joining the pile a moment later. Still holding her tight, he turned on the showerhead above the old claw foot tub. As the water pelted them, he pressed her against the back wall and made love to her, his mouth on her neck and then her breasts.

Finally, when he thought he would burst, he lifted her legs onto his hips and drove himself into her with an urgency that seemed primal and greedy, a need that could never be filled. He felt as though he could love this woman until the day he died and never get enough of her. And by her impatient thrusts he knew she felt the same.

His kisses were deep and copied the rhythm of their bodies, eliciting groans of pleasure from Nicole that carried above the steady spray of water. His breathing escalated with her response and he searched for a closer and tighter fit. Then, with his leg muscles screaming, he lunged one last time into her, pinning her body to the wall with his own and feeling her shudder against him.

With only his eyes Michael said what he was feeling as he gently nudged her under the shower, lathering her beautiful body slowly and thoroughly. She did the same to him before they rinsed beneath the cooling water.

Michael dried Nicole off and then himself before he wrapped them both in towels and led her to his room. He sat on the bed and tugged her toward him. She dropped her towel and came to him, the look of love in her eyes bringing him to full arousal. And within seconds he felt himself sheathed in her once again.

Nicole held him tight, her world spinning out of control. A part of her said she was being selfish, that she was making things worse. But how could anything be worse than saying goodbye?

Michael kissed her neck and whispered her name over and over in her ear. Never had she wanted to say the words *I love you* more than she did now, but she couldn't. Earlier tonight, when she thought she might never see him again, she had wished she'd told him how she felt. Now that she had another chance the words stuck in her throat. She had no right.

Their bodies rocked as one, and she never wanted it to stop. She arched her back and felt him slide deeper inside her. He was thick and hard and filled her perfectly. But it wasn't enough. She wanted more and more of him, never enough. She took his face in both of her hands and kissed him hard, his tongue mating with hers. If this had to be the last time, it would be the best. She slid her hands down his back and bottom, pulling him closer, memorizing every hard line of him, knowing that the time would come all too soon when she had nothing left but memories.

Her hunger for him was insatiable. She ground into him over and over, spurred on by his deep-throated moans of pleasure. His tongue lapped at her nipples, and her whole body shuddered. Her body was begging for release, but she held back, knowing he wouldn't stop until he satisfied her. Except she knew she would always want more.

He pumped into her faster, sensing she was close, and she gritted her teeth. But when she didn't respond he slipped his hand between them and worked magic with his fingers along with his thrusts. This was her undoing. He moved faster and faster, his breathing as hard as her own until she felt him go rigid. She clung to him, feeling tears rush down the sides of her face.

After a while he rolled them to their sides, their bodies still joined, and held her close.

It was over. There would never be another time.

She reveled in his warm embrace and savored every second. But finally exhaustion overtook her and she fell asleep locked in his arms.

Dawn's first light filtered through the window next to Michael's bed, and Nicole woke with a start as she realized where she was.

Cody! It wouldn't do for him to find them like this. She got out from under Michael's arm and started to get up. Michael caught her wrist.

"Don't go. Not yet."

"But Cody—"

"I know. Just another minute."

Hesitantly she stretched along the length of him and rested her head on his warm chest, trying desperately not to remember this part of her life was over.

He kissed her hair and said, "We're going to have to do something about this."

Yes, they would. She would have to tell him what had been on her mind. Before the sun went down on another day she would make him see the impossibility of a future together.

"What's on the agenda today?"

She couldn't look at him when she answered. "I have some more border paper to hang in the dining room. I was thinking of working on that."

"No. No work today. Go get some more sleep. Then when Cody wakes up, let's make breakfast together. Maybe pack a picnic. Drive away from the fire, up toward the foothills…just the three of us. How does that sound?"

"It sounds nice, Michael." She lifted her head and kissed him quickly on the cheek, then slid from beneath the sheets. She found the towel where she'd left it and wrapped it tightly around her before leaving the room.

Hearing nothing of Cody down the hall, she slipped into her own bed, feeling as though she hadn't slept a wink all night and eager to escape the pain in her heart.

At the doughnut shop to the north, down the road from Walter and Mabel's, the same old cronies had their daily coffee and read the morning news.

"Why look at this," one said. "Ain't that the Purple Palace…or what used to be? Look at all them women and kids hosin' down the place. Guess that fire musta come close. Says here the Malones stopped it before it got any houses. Damn good thing. Look at these other pictures, too. That fire looks pretty mean. Story says one of the Malone women took all these pictures before the paper showed up. Pretty good, don't ya think?"

The man to his right looked at the photos and chuckled. "Well, what do you know?"

"What?"

"Ain't that the young girl who used to come in here and order a doughnut hole and wait for us to put the help-wanted page down?"

"Yeah, I think you're right. Now that ya mention it, haven't seen her in months. Must be she got a job at the Palace...though I can't imagine doin' what. I heard it changed hands. Gonna make a bed and breakfast or some-thin' like that outta the place. Maybe she's cookin'. Seems like I saw her before, waitin' tables or cookin' up north a ways. You know, when they was makin' that movie near here."

He rubbed his unshaved chin. "I don't know. Just no-ticed that she always stuck to herself. Like she was shy...or maybe had somethin' to hide."

"Hmm. Did ya see all the young'uns in that one picture? Them Malones are breeding like rabbits down there. Couldn't happen to nicer folk, though. We could use more honest, hard-workin' people like them around these parts."

"Amen to that," said the waitress behind the counter. "Refill?" She held the pot above their mugs, and they mo-tioned for more. Then she turned to the stranger two stools over. "How 'bout you, sir?"

He stood, plunked a five on the counter and gave an unctuous smile. "No, thanks. I've got all I need."

They watched as the tall man hitched up his pants and strode confidently out the door.

"Who do ya suppose that was?" asked one of the men gaping after him.

The waitress stood with one hand on her hip and nar-rowed her eyes. "I don't know. He's been here off and on these past few months. Comes at different times of day. I always remember the big tippers. But that one...somethin' about him gives me the willies. Wouldn't mind if he never came back."

She watched until he slipped behind the wheel of his black Cadillac and then she turned away.

When Cody knocked on Nicole's door it seemed as though only minutes had passed since she'd fallen asleep, yet, glancing at the clock, she saw it was nearly ten. She told him to go on down to the kitchen and she would join him in a minute.

Exhausted and depressed, she found her robe and padded barefoot down the hall. Cody was already on the phone talking about the fire. He asked if he could go riding with Billy and a few others and she gave her permission. It would be easier to say what had to be said without Cody nearby.

While she fixed Cody a bowl of cereal she thought about last night. She never should have let it happen. Now what words could she use that would ever make him understand? Regardless, today was definitely the day to tell Michael she must leave. Robert would never give up. Someday he would show up and she would have to run. And when that time came Michael would be unable to go with her. No matter how many ways she looked at it, there was no happy ending in sight.

Cody had no sooner finished eating and getting dressed than Billy came and whisked him off. Nicole sat brooding over a second cup of coffee when Michael ambled into the kitchen, freshly showered and dressed.

At the mere sight of him, it was all she could do not to cry. He was such a good man. How could she bring herself to hurt him? He'd done nothing to deserve it.

She made him his favorite scrambled eggs with cheese while he helped himself to coffee and sat at the table. As long as the conversation centered on the events of the previous day Nicole held together. But when he told her how he had finally worked through his anger with Max and his mom and even Roxanne, and that trusting women was no longer an issue, Nicole felt the last threads of control slip away. Tears trailing down her cheeks, she walked to the sink and rinsed out her coffee cup.

Michael came up behind her and laid his hands on her shoulders. "Is something wrong?"

"Deprive an emotional female of sleep and look what happens," she said. She reached up and lay one hand on his. "I'm sorry, Michael. I'm happy for you. Truly I am."

"You want to go back to bed for a while?"

She kept her back to him and dried the cup, glancing at the clock above the stove. Cody would be back around two. There wasn't a lot of time. "No. Just let me shower and get dressed. Then we can get ready for our picnic, okay?"

He kissed the nape of her neck. "Take as long as you'd like. I'll clean up here."

Sixteen

It was just past noon when they began to prepare their picnic. Michael was putting a few things into a basket while Nicole stood at the kitchen sink washing fruit and worrying about the day ahead. Since they were leaving later than planned, they wouldn't have as much time alone, which in some ways suited her fine. What she had to say would be painful; prolonging it would be sheer torture.

Looking out the window, she blinked back the tears and said, "It's so nice out. What would you say about walking a short way to the stream…instead of taking the van to the mountains?"

Michael put a bottle of wine into the basket. "Whatever your heart desires."

Her heart desired a lifetime with this man. Something she couldn't have. But worse than her own devastation would be the pain she was about to cause him. He hadn't said he loved her, but she knew.

She finished at the sink, and then they walked less than a mile north of the house. They found a shady spot between two aspens along the fast-moving stream, where rocks had worn slick and shone brightly under the vast blue sky. The setting was perfect, Nicole thought sadly as she helped Michael spread a blanket. Too perfect for bad news. It should be a day and place to celebrate life…and love. She let out a ragged sigh, knowing the time was near.

After sharing a pair of binoculars to scan the horizon, they sat on the blanket, and Michael extracted two goblets from the basket, filling each with wine.

He held his glass high and said, ''To the love of my life,'' and she clinked her glass to his, finding it ironic that he would use that word for the first time today. They locked eyes as they drank and Nicole thought her heart would break. It was time to tell him. She started to speak but he pressed a finger to her lips and smiled at her.

''Remember I said we had to do something about our sleeping arrangements? Well, there's only one solution I can think of.''

She held her breath, praying he wouldn't deepen the hole she'd already dug for herself. But then he said what she had only dared dream, and what she feared most.

''I love you, Nicole. I think I've loved you from the first second I laid eyes on you—standing on my front porch in those ridiculous high heels and ratty blond hair.''

She wanted to say *I love you, too,* but how could she? He would never understand.

He set his glass down and reached for both of her hands. She could feel herself trembling as she blinked hard to hold back her emotions. *Please, God, help me. How do I spare this good man more pain? Please don't let him ask me to—* Her mind raced, then came to a screeching halt when she thought about Friday. He'd flown off with Josh and had been gone most of the day, far too long to simply buy paint. *Oh, please, God, no…*

"Michael, I—"

"Shh." He cupped his hand over her mouth. "Please, Nicole. There's more."

She felt sick to her stomach. She had waited too long.

Michael raised her hands to his lips and kissed them softly, and then he met her eyes. "I want to marry you, Nicole. I want to spend the rest of my life here with you and Cody…and if you want, more children, too."

She closed her eyes, the world tilting on its axis.

"You know it will be hard work—managing a B&B—and we'll never be rich, not in money terms, anyway. But in every other way, I'll give you everything within my power to make you happy."

She couldn't stop the flow of tears any longer. As he brushed them away tenderly, she wanted to tell him how perfect his proposal was, how she longed for nothing more than what he offered. She gazed deep into his intense blue eyes and saw the most loving soul, offering itself to her and only her…forever, and she wanted to die for what could have been.

"Michael—" she started, then pushing past the pain she choked out the rest. "I'm sorry, Michael, but I can't marry you."

On the ride back to the Palace, Cody watched Billy as he dismounted and examined the leg of his paint pony. "Is he okay?"

Billy worked his hands systematically down the pony's leg and then lifted his hoof. "Thank goodness. It's just a bad shoe."

"Can you still ride him?" Cody asked.

Billy shielded his eyes from the sun with the side of his hand and studied the valley below. They were about a half mile south of the Palace. He tethered his horse to a tree near the ridge and said, "I'll ride with you and then walk back."

"Gee, that's a long walk."

Billy settled his hat lower on his forehead. "Yep. It will be for my pony, too. But hey, it's a beautiful day. I don't mind." He nudged Cody's foot from the stirrup, stepped into it and flung himself up into the saddle behind Cody. Cody giggled as they began their slow descent to the freshly painted house.

Nicole had said she and Michael were driving the van up into the foothills, so when Billy spotted both vehicles in the drive, he changed his mind and pulled up on the reins. "I just remembered some things I have to do at the ranch. Mind walking the rest of the way and letting me borrow your horse?"

"Sure." Cody slid to the ground.

"I'll wait until you get inside."

"It's okay. You can go."

"Nah. I'll wait. Talk to ya later, big guy."

"See ya," Cody said, starting to skip after a few yards. When he reached the porch he turned and waved.

Billy waved his hat high in the air and then rode off toward his lame pony.

Nicole found the shock on Michael's face swift and painful to watch.

"What are you saying, Nicole?" he asked, jaw muscles clenched.

"Cody and I are leaving this week."

Fury flared his nostrils and set his mouth in a grim, straight line. "Did you plan to tell me? Or would I just wake up one morning and find you gone?"

She couldn't blame him for being angry. "No. I planned on telling you today."

He shot her an incredulous look. "And last night? What was that? One last romp for the road?"

"I tried to stop you, but—"

"Why?" he interrupted. "Why do you have to leave?"

"Robert. Sooner or later he'll find us and—"

"And you don't trust me to protect you."

"You can't watch over us twenty-four hours a day, Michael."

He pushed off the blanket and glared down at her. "And who's going to watch over you at all if you leave?" He grabbed her roughly by the arms and pulled her up to him. "Tell me."

Breaking free of his grasp she turned her back on him, feeling her own temper and self-control slipping. "That's not the point."

"Then what is?" he shouted to her back.

"You want—you deserve a wife. Someone who can put down roots like you have. I can't do that, Michael. If I hear Robert is anywhere near here I'd have to run. You don't know him. He'd take Cody in a heartbeat and I'd never see my son again." She stared across the field of wildflowers at the Palace, a proud monument to Michael's hard work. "You deserve someone who can live in that beautiful house with you forever. And I'm just not—" Her focus narrowed and her heart pumped faster in her chest. "Oh, God. No! Please, no!" she shouted louder.

Michael came alongside her, hands planted firmly on his hips. "What is it?"

"There!" She pointed a shaky finger. "Black Cadillac. It's him."

She set out at a dead run, flying over uneven terrain. Fifty yards, a hundred. Much more ground ahead of her than behind. Another dozen yards and she lost her footing, stumbled and fell. Pain seared through her hands and knees.

She came up gasping for air, Michael right beside her, taking her hand.

"You go on," she said, winded. "But be careful. He may have a gun." Michael started off and she called after him. "If Cody's in that car, call the sheriff. Tell him to look for a black Cadillac...about nine years old...Campbell. Robert Campbell."

Michael sprinted the rest of the way. Nicole ignored the stitch in her side and ran as fast as she could. Still, the house seemed miles away. Finally she reached the back door and stumbled in. Michael hung up the phone and started pacing.

"Where is he?" She spun around, half crazed. "Please tell me he's here."

Michael went to her and held her, a different kind of pain etched on his face than the one she'd seen just minutes before. "A deputy is on the way."

"His horse! Did you check—"

"I called the ranch. Billy said he left Cody on the hill. He watched until he was in the house."

"Oh, no. Oh, God. Please, no." She paced to the door and back, adrenaline pumping. She didn't know what to do. "Maybe we should try to catch up with him. Did you see what direction he headed?"

Michael shook his head. "No. And we can't leave now. The deputy should be here any minute."

"I'll go, then. You wait here."

He grabbed her by both shoulders. "You'll do no such thing. What would you do if you found him? You said he was probably armed."

"Oh, Michael, I can't just stand here and—" She heard the siren coming up the drive and a car screeching to a stop outside the door. She flew outside, hoping against hope that Cody would be there, that her worst nightmare would be over.

The deputy stepped slowly from the car. Alone.

Nicole slumped back against Michael. Impatiently she answered more questions about Robert. When she finished, the deputy called it in and an APB went out for one Robert Campbell.

"Not too many black Caddies around these parts, ma'am. I'm sure we'll find him. He couldn't have gotten very far."

Then the idea came to her. "What about Josh?" The deputy gave her a blank stare. "He's got a plane. He could fly over…maybe spot it."

"I'll call him," Michael said, racing back inside.

"In the meantime, ma'am, why don't you wait here. You never know. He might call."

She doubted it, but Nicole went in anyway, inviting the deputy to join her for what she hoped would be a short wait.

With Josh's help, the Cadillac was spotted a couple of hours later. Campbell was pulled over just outside of Livingston. Alone. There was no evidence of Cody having been with him, although a suitcase of boy's clothing with tags still attached made Campbell's intentions quite clear.

While he maintained that he never saw the boy, his angry protests were met with a speedy arrest. Not only was there a shotgun on the back seat—a clear violation of his parole—but the amount of cocaine found under the seat was enough to prove he was dealing again.

The deputy relayed all this to Nicole and Michael when the call came, assuring them that Robert was no longer a threat, that he would be put away for a very long time.

But, still, where was Cody? How did they know Robert didn't put him somewhere or harm him?

Michael sat on the steps of the porch, his hands hanging limp between his legs. All of the Malones had congregated on the front porch awaiting assignments. The Palace and Malone property had been divided into grids with pairs of people ready to search every inch of ground. Billy stood off by himself, his chin on his chest. Michael watched as Max approached him.

"Want to go with me and look for Cody?"

Billy turned slowly, his face racked with guilt. "Sure, Grandpa."

Michael eyed the old dinner bell that hung from a post in the yard. Up until now he'd viewed it as an interesting decoration. Now he knew it would serve a purpose. He stood and walked down the steps and, joining the others, he said, "As soon as one of you finds Cody, rush back here, and we'll ring the bell for the rest of you to return. Just in case you don't hear it, call back here every half hour."

Teams scattered in all directions, leaving Nicole alone with Michael. "I don't think I can bear it," she said, burying her face in her hands. "I'd rather be out there searching than here doing nothing."

The anger Michael had felt earlier had been replaced with worry and a big dose of guilt. Nicole had been right. He hadn't been able to protect her. He crossed to her and took her in his arms. "I know, sweetheart. But this way you'll be here when they find him."

"You really think they will? What if Robert—"

"Don't even go there. Cody's around. I'm sure of it. Remember how you used to tell him to hide if he ever saw the bad man in the Cadillac? I bet that's exactly what he's doing."

"Oh, Michael. I hope you're right. It's getting dark out. We have to find him."

A few long hours later they heard a car speed up the drive. Max stepped out from behind the wheel of his Suburban. From the opposite side walked Billy…holding Cody's hand.

Nicole ran the last few yards and knelt before her son, feeling the warmth of his small body next to hers. "Cody, Cody." She held him close and kissed his cool cheek.

"Mama! I was sooo scared. But I hid…just like you told me."

"My brave young man. I love you, Cody."

Max moved closer and felt his forehead. "He seems to be okay, but maybe I should check him over before we leave."

"Of course," Nicole said, taking Cody inside and setting him down on the sofa. Outside she heard Billy ringing the bell, and the joy in her heart sang nearly as loudly. Her baby was safe. And Robert was in custody. She said a prayer of thanksgiving as Max examined her son. Thanksgiving that Cody was okay, thanksgiving for the love of a good man and thanksgiving for the best extended family a person could ever hope for.

And next to her stood Michael, her rock, the man who was just as relieved with Cody's safe return and Robert's internment as she was. But when she remembered her rejection of his proposal, and the pain she had caused him, the tears came once again.

As if he'd read her thoughts, Michael wrapped his arms around her, and she clung to him.

Soon Max rose from the sofa and directed them both toward the door. "Besides a few insect bites, he seems perfectly fine…physically," he whispered. "But keep an eye on him for a while. It's been quite a trauma for such a little guy. Maybe over the next few days you might encourage him to talk about it, tell you how he's feeling."

Nicole could see how Max was feeling. The past forty-eight hours had obviously taken their toll on him. He looked weary beyond measure. Not wanting to keep him another moment she gave him a quick hug and thanked him, then returned to Cody's side, leaving Max alone with Michael. Out of the corner of her eye, Nicole watched, wondering what else might happen on this emotionally charged day.

Michael stood with his hands in his pockets, his head bent. Tentatively Max placed a hand on Michael's shoulder and then suddenly pulled him close. "You have a beautiful home, Michael," he said over his son's shoulder. "And an even more beautiful little family. I hope you'll have many years of happiness here." Max started to leave, but before he could, Michael tugged him back and returned his father's warm embrace.

Nicole felt another tear slide down the side of her nose. Tonight was indeed a night for miracles.

Seventeen

With Cody tucked safely in bed, Nicole joined Michael on the porch, feeling every bit as exhausted as Michael looked, yet floating on a cloud of peace and possibilities. He was leaning back in the swing, hands locked behind his head, staring at the starry sky. She sat down beside him, trying not to interrupt his reverie. She hadn't forgotten the question that had hung over them since this afternoon, but at the moment she was more than satisfied to simply enjoy the serenity that was so uniquely a Montana night.

Eventually Michael draped his arm behind her and let out a long sigh. "Well?" he asked, looking at her with a weary smile.

"Well what?" she asked, feeling suddenly playful.

"Are you ready to give me a different answer?"

She shook her head slowly. "No, I'm not," she started, thinking she'd tease him a little longer. When his smile started to fade, she spoke quickly, deciding tonight was not a night for games. "There's something I have to tell you first."

He sat up and rested his elbows on his knees, looking for all the world as though she were preparing to drop another bomb.

She scooted closer and took his hand. "I have to tell you something that I've been holding back for far too long, that I didn't think I had the right or freedom to say until today." She stroked his long, loving fingers, then gazed up at him.

"I love you, Michael…more than I ever thought I could."

He pulled her into his arms and exhaled over her head. "Nicole, Nicole. You scared the hell out of me. I thought there was still a problem."

She looked up at him and touched his cheek. "I think we've had enough problems to last a lifetime, don't you?"

"Probably so. And as the years go by we'll probably have more. But as long as we face them together there's nothing we can't handle." He held her at arm's length now and smiled tenderly. "Does this mean…?"

"Yes," she said softly. "I accept."

He kissed her gently on the lips and then pulled her onto his lap as he had the first time they'd sat there together. After a moment he said, "We'll have to go into Bozeman for a ring."

Nicole looked at him to see if it was his turn to tease her, but he didn't appear to be playing it coy. "You mean you haven't already got one?"

"No. I thought you'd rather pick one out yourself. Are you disappointed?"

Was she? Maybe a little. "It's just that I thought I had it all figured out. About Friday, I mean. You and Josh were gone so long, I thought maybe—"

"Ah, that," he said, a smug smile curving his lips. He reached into his pocket, and for a second she thought maybe he had a ring after all and was just having fun with her. But when his hand came out, it was holding an envelope, not a small box.

He handed it to her and her eyes fixed on her name written in the familiar hand. "Michael...what is this?"

"Just one more bend in our roller-coaster weekend. Go ahead. Open it."

She broke the seal slowly, her fingers beginning to shake.

Our dearest Nicole,

How do we begin to say how sorry we are for letting this happen, for all the years that have kept us apart?

When we read about Robert's trial we tried to find you, but it was as though you had disappeared into thin air. We know now we shouldn't have waited that long. We miss you so, sweetheart. And now your young man, Michael, tells us you have a wonderful young son. To think we have a grandson we have never seen breaks our hearts.

Michael told us that you both are well and safe. We are grateful for that, and we were most pleased to hear that this fine young man plans to ask you to marry him. We would never presume to interfere in your life, dear, but should you accept his proposal, we want you to know we will be very happy for you.

Nicole, do you think you could find it in your heart to forgive us? We would so love to see you and Cody. And if there is a wedding, we would love to help you with it or at least be there to wish you well.

Dearest, there hasn't been a day that we haven't regretted our actions, that we haven't blamed ourselves for driving you into such a painful ordeal. We are both so very, very sorry.

With all our love, now and always,

Mom and Dad

Nicole reread the letter, until the words started to blur. Then she carefully folded the pages and put them back into the envelope. She blinked hard and gazed up at this dear man who held her close. "Michael, I don't know what to say. How did you—?"

"Easy. Went to the library and used the Internet. Did a search using your maiden name and then your mother's. They live in Arizona now."

"How…how can I ever thank you?"

"Shh." He bent his head and kissed her softly. "You already have. You've agreed to marry me."

She snuggled under his arm, listening to the crickets and feeling utterly loved.

"Amazing how things have changed for both of us in one short summer," he said. "You stumbled onto this place with no idea what would happen. And me? Well, when I first arrived here the Malones were pretty much strangers to me. I thought they were all looking at me as…as…I don't know. Maybe the unknown Malone, the bastard son. I just wanted them to see me as Michael Phillips, a man with his own family, his own history.

"But after the last couple days—" he dragged his hand through his hair "—I don't know whether they see me as a Malone or a Phillips now. Maybe a little of both. Which, of course, I am."

He seemed shocked at his own choice of words. "I've never said that out loud before. And you know? It doesn't sound all bad." He straightened his back and smiled. "I guess I could be a whole lot worse than a Malone."

Nicole felt tears burn her eyes. "Yes. I think you could. You have a wonderful family, Michael."

"And so do you."

"I know. They treat me as one of their own, and I sincerely appreciate it."

"That's true, but it's not what I meant."

She looked at the letter clutched in her hand. There was no decision to be made where her parents were concerned. She had taken responsibility for her actions and forgiven them years ago. Soon she would see them, and Cody would have the grandparents he'd been denied for so long.

"We're very lucky...you and I," she said after a while. "We both have two families who truly care about us."

Michael said, "Uh-huh," into her neck and then wrapped his arms tighter around her. "So what do you think?"

"About what?"

"Assuming we can get rings and all our families together, is Labor Day weekend too soon for a wedding?"

She looked over her shoulder, flashing him her best shocked expression. "You mean we have to wait *that* long?"

His laugh was loud, his breath warming her down to her toes. But then she heard a squeak behind her and she turned. Cody stood in the doorway looking very small and frightened.

"Come here, sweetheart. What's wrong? Another bad dream?"

He lifted himself up on the swing and shook his head. "I wasn't sleeping yet. I was thinking about that man. What if he comes back?"

Michael answered. "He's not coming back, Cody. You'll be out of school and all grown-up before he ever gets out of jail."

Cody hung his head, still troubled about something. "I wish he wasn't my father," he said softly.

At a loss for words Nicole gave him an understanding hug while Michael eased her aside and walked over to Cody. He hunkered down next to the boy and waited until he looked up. "I have something to ask you."

Cody eyed him curiously.

"Since you're the man of your family I thought I should probably ask your permission."

Cody wiggled forward, looking more interested. "About what?"

Michael glanced at Nicole and she nodded with a smile.

"I would like to marry your mom, if it's all right with you."

"Really?"

"Really."

His little eyebrows shot straight up. "Then we can stay here forever and ever?"

"Forever and ever."

Cody threw himself into Michael's arms as Nicole wiped away another tear.

Michael said, "Well? You didn't answer my question."

Cody pulled back and jumped up and down with each "Yes, yes, yes." Then he stopped and said, "I wish you were my real dad."

"That's something else I wanted to ask you about. What if I were to adopt you?"

"Is that like what Ryder did to Billy?" His eyes were big as saucers.

"Exactly."

Cody turned around and looked at his mom. "Is it my birthday or something?"

Nicole and Michael laughed as Cody scooted over and Michael sat beside him. Cody looked from one adult to the other and then he wrinkled his nose. "Is this the part where you guys get all mushy and stuff?"

They laughed louder, and Nicole nudged him off the swing. "Off to bed, young man."

Nicole watched him run inside, expecting it would be some time until he fell asleep. But that was all right. He had a lot of new things to think about now.

And, thank God, they were all good.

Nicole nuzzled her head under Michael's chin, and he brushed his lips against her hair. "So, my love, where do you want the ceremony?" he asked.

She thought only a moment, then she wrapped her arms around his waist and smiled.

"Right here on the porch...where we fell in love."

* * * * *

Don't miss Silhouette's newest cross-line promotion,

Four royal sisters find their own Prince Charmings as they embark on separate journeys to find their missing brother, the Crown Prince!

Royally Wed

The search begins in October 1999 and continues through February 2000:

On sale October 1999: **A ROYAL BABY ON THE WAY**
by award-winning author **Susan Mallery** (Special Edition)

On sale November 1999: **UNDERCOVER PRINCESS**
by bestselling author **Suzanne Brockmann** (Intimate Moments)

On sale December 1999: **THE PRINCESS'S WHITE KNIGHT**
by popular author **Carla Cassidy** (Romance)

On sale January 2000: **THE PREGNANT PRINCESS**
by rising star **Anne Marie Winston** (Desire)

On sale February 2000: **MAN...MERCENARY...MONARCH**
by top-notch talent **Joan Elliott Pickart** (Special Edition)

ROYALLY WED
Only in—
SILHOUETTE BOOKS

Available at your favorite retail outlet.

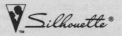

Visit us at www.romance.net

SSERW

If you enjoyed what you just read,
then we've got an offer you can't resist!

Take 2 bestselling love stories FREE!

Plus get a FREE surprise gift!

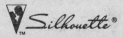

COMING NEXT MONTH